Walk the Night

Walk the Night

a novel
of gays
in the
Holocaust,
by

Robert C. Reinhart

Boston ♦ Alyson Publications, Inc.

The characters in this book are fictional, but the facts about Nazi Germany, the laws against gays, the concentration camps, and postwar Germany are not. They are disturbingly real.

Typeset and printed in the United States of America.

This is a trade paperback original from Alyson Publications, Inc., 40 Plympton Street, Boston, Massachusetts 02118.

First edition: October 1994

5 4 3 2 1

ISBN 1-55583-267-9

Library of Congress Cataloging-in-Publication Data
Reinhart, Robert C.
    Walk the night : a novel of gays in the Holocaust / by Robert C. Reinhart. – 1st ed.
        p.   cm.
    ISBN 1-55583-267-9 (trade) : $9.95
    1. Gay men–Germany–Berlin–Fiction.   2. World War, 1939–1945-
-Germany–Berlin–Fiction.   3. Holocaust, Jewish (1939–1945)-
-Fiction.   4. Fathers and sons–Fiction.   5. Berlin (Germany)-
-Fiction.   I. Title.
PS3568.E4924W35   1994
813'.54–dc20   94-29726

My affectionate thanks to Dr. Leah Schaefer for helping me find my own past and a surprise ending, and to Herbert Bott, my fine and encouraging friend.

And for Ivan Pattison, Nick Frank, and too many other loved and valued friends lost to AIDS.

Observations & acknowledgments

While entire libraries are dedicated to chronicles of the Second World War, Nazi Germany, the Holocaust, and the concentration camps, books on what happened to homosexuals caught up in those events would fill only a couple of inches of shelf space. To paraphrase Edna St. Vincent Millay, "the presence of their absence is everywhere." There is little to read about gays in that country and era, and what there is inclines one to conclude that the omission results as much from prudery as from a lack of easily accessible or verifiable information. The behavior of the Allies and the German government after the war strongly suggests that both surmises are true.

Current research shows that tens of thousands of gays died in the Holocaust. Under the circumstances, such a "numbers game" may seem tawdry, but the much lower numbers often cited badly skew any consideration of the dimensions of the crime and the dedicated viciousness with which it was executed.

It is often said that those who do not remember the past are doomed to relive it. But what's to be done when there is almost no past to remember?

For what little information there is to rely on, I am particularly grateful to Heinz Heger's account of concentration-camp life for gays in his *The Men with the Pink Triangle,* my original source of interest and inspiration. Also, my sincere thanks to Richard Plant for spending time talking with me and for his book *The Pink Triangle.* And I thank Frank Rector for his *The Nazi Extermination of Homosexuals* with its information on Weimar nightlife and the arts. The material Leda reads in chapter 1 from C.R. Doyle's *Missing from the Holocaust: Forgotten Nazi Victims* is a historical summary created for this book.

Robert C. Reinhart
May 1994

I am thy father's spirit,
Doom'd for a certain time to walk the night,
And for the day confin'd to fast in fires,
Till the foul crimes done in my day of nature
Are burnt and purg'd away. But that I am forbid
To tell the secrets of my prison-house,
I could a tale unfold whose lightest word
Would harrow up thy soul, freeze thy young blood,
Make thy two eyes, like stars, start from their spheres,
Thy knotted and combined locks to part,
And each particular hair to stand on end,
Like quills upon the fretful porpentine,
But this eternal blazon must not be
To ears of flesh and blood. List, list, oh list!
— THE GHOST OF HAMLET'S FATHER
IN SHAKESPEARE'S *HAMLET*,
ACT I, SCENE 4

National hatred is something peculiar. You will
always find it strongest and most violent where there
is the lowest degree of culture.
—JOHANN WOLFGANG VON GOETHE

The only thing necessary for the triumph of evil
is for good men to do nothing.
—EDMUND BURKE

Leda's Story

New York, 1974
Berlin, 1934

Chapter 1

His mother was indestructible. If that wasn't true, what was?
Wasn't she Leda Kohl, world-famous pianist?

All the emergency trips to the hospital, riding with her in
ambulances bullying their way through Manhattan traffic
couldn't convince him otherwise. Starchy nurses, the medici-
nal stink of the house, and scowling doctors all told the truth,
but he wanted none of it.

Facts that he dodged, she confronted. She insisted on having everything explained to her. She made them show her the
X rays and decipher the omens of her entrails. She insisted on
knowing what would truly help her condition or merely pro-
long the inevitable, and was often of two minds about which
she wanted.

This woman who had once disdained aspirin now gulped
painkillers and accepted needles with obvious gratitude. What
little of this Paul happened to see he found distressing. He
averted his eyes and his mind.

Then the shift in the balance between days spent in the
hospital and days at home began. The hospital was winning
this numbers game.

For Paul, the days veered wildly between unfounded hope
and despair. But, as anyone knows who has ever tended the

gravely sick or dying, daily life often seems like a plotless black comedy. The deadly drama sometimes took absurdist turns.

There was the day Leda once again returned from the hospital and casually mentioned to Maria one of her first lovely memories of America: canned yellow freestone peaches with their raggedy red hearts. The housekeeper had immediately set out to find them. Nine stores and three hours later, Paul found Maria sobbing at the kitchen table. "All Madame wants in this world is canned yellow freestone peaches and I can't even do that for her. When she needs me most, I fail her." Paul calmed Maria by promising to help her find the peaches. Later, when he asked his mother if she still had her heart set on the peaches, she'd looked at him queerly and said, "What peaches?"

Life became full of such tangled intentions, of hope misspent and despair denied.

Two weeks before the onset of his mother's intestinal cancer, Paul moved back to this house he'd grown up in. He was nearing the end of a rapidly advancing divorce that would end a sixteen-year marriage. He'd been dating a woman who, if he'd been able to see it, was much like the one he was divorcing. As his mother's illness claimed more of his time, the woman started to drift out of his life. Her own mother had died a year earlier after a three-year decline, and she knew how illness could subsume every other interest. She couldn't face seeing Paul through another, or postponing more of her life for someone else. Besides, he still hadn't taken her to bed and she didn't want to wait on a man who had such wrongheaded respect for her.

The house lent an air of lunacy to looking after Leda, as there were few direct routes from place to place. It was an inherited stone pile just off Fifth Avenue on East Sixty-third Street and was built to be run by seven or eight servants, but now there was only Maria who, at seventy-three, was fifteen years Leda's senior. Maria was slow, fragile, and forgetful, but faithful in her attentions to Leda.

Leda had been moved to the large first-floor sitting room where, over the past four months, all kinds of rented hospital equipment had been added. The equipment arrived to answer a crisis and stayed. Piece by piece, it elbowed aside the fine furniture that was shifted to a corner and covered with dust sheets. Leda called the shrouded pile "the ghost of pleasures past." The wholly utilitarian was ousting the merely beautiful.

Nurses arrived for only the briefest of stays. Leda hated the sight of all their bustling efficiency in a home where there had been colorful people and so much vitality.

Missing most noticeably from the room was music. Leda found it too painful to be reduced to a passive listener and she could no longer sit at a piano. Her fingers were still supple and, alone, she would tap out pieces silently on the blanket, hearing them in her mind.

If Paul worked at denial, his mother labored to make him foresee a future without her. She insisted on putting her affairs in order and he found her clearheaded instructions amazing, considering the quantity of mind-bending medications she took.

He spent hours taking notes on legal pads and feeling squeamish as she dictated bequests, emptying onto paper the five floors full of forty years of living. Her beloved collections of Meissen, Limoges, and Spode would be scattered across the world to friends, the good furniture would pass through Sotheby's salesrooms, and the indifferent lot of paintings and drawings would be taken for disposal by the gallery that had sold most of them to her.

These sessions were long and only moderately productive, as there were stories associated with many of the pieces and

Paul had often been with Leda when she acquired them. On worldwide concert tours, she would kidnap Paul from his current tutor and take him to museums, shopping, or to meals with interesting people. She would say, "This is your real education, Paul. However, the law insists you be crammed with information you will seldom use and soon forget. Seeing the world and something of life is how fortunate people are truly educated."

Paul, of course, could have first claim on everything in the house, but he couldn't bring himself to admit he wanted any of it, because that would be to acknowledge the means of acquisition.

He'd once asked her, "How do you remember all this stuff, where it is?" and she'd said, "I got acquainted with loss early and the awful mess it leaves when it's not seen to properly. I've never lived in dread of dying, I knew my day would come, so I've thought about how I'd like my affairs managed. Don't you ever think of it?"

He wanted to say, "Not until now," but didn't. Leda would be his first loss. His father had died during World War II when Paul was too young to take the measure of grief.

"I'd just leave the lot to you, Paul, but what would you do with it all? This house will have to go, so where would you put it? This place has been unmanageable for years and, without Maria, it will be impossible. The joint is laid out like a fun house. Besides, you don't have children and soon you won't even have a wife." Paul winced.

She put an apologetic hand on Paul's shoulder and said, "That came out wrong. I'm sorry. What I mean is that I would wish you a family, especially now. It's selfish of me but, even under the circumstances, it's good to have you here again."

She remembered so well where everything in the house was, because she wandered it at night when her energy allowed. The painkillers now worked for only a half hour or so, and she used the dark to do things she wasn't permitted when others were around to make her behave herself. She didn't worry about being heard by Paul and Maria, as both slept soundly behind massive walnut doors.

Managing stairs was dangerous but, so far, she'd gotten away with it, and it pleased her to still be able to put one over, to feel there was still some life and mischief in the old girl. It was better than just lying there and letting pain have its way. She even managed to wend her way to the kitchen where she would make herself a gin martini and smoke one of the cigarettes she kept hidden in the silver cupboard, small lovely luxuries denied her by sensible caretakers.

Most importantly, it was good to be alone and have room to think. There was almost always somebody in the sitting room acting solicitous or insisting on doing something for her. She'd given up resisting the unrelenting care. It took too much energy. Alone, she could review and plan, and spend a little time with her ghosts.

There was so much for her to sort out and, of most pressing importance, one immense question to settle, one painful truth she now longed to tell. She had decided she owed a large debt to the past, but was baffled about how to pay it. She only knew she must try.

These days, she often felt she was losing the present to the past, as Rudy and Dieter started reaching across time and asserting their claim, becoming more real, as the present grew less so. Forty years gone and now Rudy and Dieter were again vibrantly alive, evoking the joy and terror that had been a part of her life with them in Berlin forty years ago.

She had turned her back on Nazi Germany and never looked back, never returned, until now. And she could have gone back in glory, could have taken the fortunes they offered her to tour, but the lavish offers seemed like bribes, and she felt that returning would have been like saying, "All is forgiven." Nothing was forgiven and never could be.

She had even rejected the language. As soon as she could master the most rudimentary English she spoke nothing else and, in one of their few major arguments, had forbidden Paul to study it. "It is a perverted language, good only for making the monstrous commonplace. I won't have you learning it!" she shrieked, then began to sob. Where her argument might not have dissuaded Paul, her tears did, because they were eloquent of anguish.

Now, feeling the limits of mortality, she again looked at her long-ignored past and thought of Paul's father, wondered how to tell Paul the truth about the lovely man.

She spent weeks on the question and got nowhere near an answer to a question that was too "damned if you do, damned if you don't" until she thought, Well, I wouldn't think about how to play a piece. I'd work on it, master it, find out what made it tick.

She decided to exhume her past completely and work to rediscover what had driven and shaped it. Perhaps it hadn't been as terrifying as she remembered. She would also call her lawyer and find out how to leave money for someone who had almost certainly been killed.

⸎

"Leda, my dear, you can't leave a half million dollars to someone you think is dead. I can't begin to tell you what a mess that could make of your estate. It could tie that money up for years."

"Paul would still have plenty, wouldn't he, Prescott?"

"Of course but, for all practical purposes, there'd be a half million in what would amount to escrow, not earning a cent, the estate committed to following a trail that may well lead nowhere. All that money might even attract unscrupulous people. Perhaps if you explained it to me more fully..."

"Not until I talk to Paul. But I can't do that until I sort things out. Truth is, I've started feeling guilty about the past. Not that I could have done more than I did. But I still feel like a coward for running away. I tried. I honestly did."

She stopped. "I'm not making much sense, am I?"

"Don't upset yourself, Leda."

"It's time I was upset. I should have been more upset years ago. Now when I talk to Paul it will look like a deathbed confession."

"What will?"

"None of your business. And don't mention any of this to Paul."

⁊

It had been a difficult and upsetting day. Facts about his mother's condition had invaded his office and it was no longer a haven from hard truth. Paul hadn't been able to get much done but, instead of leaving, by late afternoon he was still in his office, immobilized by confusion.

The day had begun with a call from an editor of the *New York Times* obituary department.

"Hi," the man began. "We're trying to find someone to help us update our information on Leda Kohl."

"Who is this?" Paul had asked.

"I'm sorry. This is Albin Krebs over at the *Times.*"

"This office manages Leda Kohl. Would you like me to send you the biography we use?"

"I've got one dated March 13 of this year."

"That's the latest. Why are you interested now?"

"Someone in our arts department called to say we should update."

Oh, God, Paul thought, but said levelly, "Of course."

"I think the picture we have is an old one. Is there a recent one?"

"The one we sent with the press release was taken last December. If you have it there, look on the back."

"Says, 'December 1973.'"

"That's the most recent."

"She's fifty-eight."

"She always looked a great deal younger." The past tense had slipped out and Paul winced.

"She had a son. Is he still living?"

"Yes. His name's Paul."

"Paul Kohl?"

"Paul Howe. His father was Farragut Howe. He was killed during World War II at the Battle of Leyte Gulf. He was awarded a DSC. Would you like more information on him?"

"That's enough. We'll have him on file."

Paul was disappointed. He still respected his father's heroic history, and wished he had more than scraps of memory or anecdotes he'd overheard in childhood. As a child, the walls of his room had been covered with maps of Pacific sea battles, his shelves filled with books on naval wars and the models he had built of famous military ships. It was only during his own time in the navy that Paul's regard for military heroism lost its luster. But his memory of his father still retained its glow of heroism.

"I have an old article from *Collier's* that says Howe and Leda Kohl met and married in Berlin in 1935. Right?"

"Yes."

"And their only child was born shortly after they returned to the States?"

"In January of 1936."

"Kohl was a lot younger than Howe."

"Thirty years or so."

"Was she running from the Nazis?"

"Nothing that dramatic. Mr. Howe put her under contract and brought her to America. Then they married and she stayed."

"The year?"

"'Thirty-five. I'll check it, to be sure. Miss Kohl never speaks of that period."

The man asked more questions and Paul managed to answer in an even voice, while his sweating palms told him how he felt.

Shortly after Krebs's call, Leda's lawyer phoned.

"I don't mean to upset you, Paul, but I was curious about your mother's medication."

"Which one? There are about a dozen. Why are you asking?"

"She hasn't signed her will, and if she keeps changing it, she won't." Then, realizing his comment might have inflicted pain, he amended, "That came out wrong, Paul, but it does concern me that her medications might be interfering with her judgment."

"Her judgment is excellent. She amazes me. I'm the one getting everything backwards these days. What's she want?"

"She wants to leave a great deal of money to someone she was pretty sure died."

"Who?"

"She won't say. She's apparently started to feel this person isn't dead. She says they're very much alive in her dreams. Probably the pills, but..."

"Man or woman?"

"She didn't say."

"If what she wants won't tie us up in probate, let her have her way. Why not?"

"It makes matters very untidy."

Paul didn't give a damn, but knew it was useless to say so. "Should I speak to Mother?"

"Please don't, Paul. I wasn't supposed to call you."

Then why the hell did you? Paul thought as he hung up.

Well, why shouldn't his mother leave her money however she wanted? There was more than enough, and he would probably never be able to track down all there was.

He returned to his effort to update the catalog of his mother's more than four hundred recordings that were still available worldwide, a daunting effort, as contracts crossed dozens of borders, were in fifteen languages, and were scattered over sixty labels of various nationalities. The task was further complicated by the use of her works in anthologies.

His mother's career was his occupation, and he kept a small office in Rockefeller Center with just enough room for himself and a secretary who came in three days a week. She was a so-so typist and abrupt on the phone, but she spoke four languages and that made her invaluable.

The door read, "Kohl Management," and, until the last few weeks, it had been the entrance to an extremely busy place, as his mother spent forty weeks a year concertizing around the world. As word of her illness spread, calls for bookings became infrequent.

He began wondering about keeping the office. What work there'd be could probably be done from home ... wherever that might turn out to be.

He was finally able to rouse himself and leave his office, but as he walked home he kept coming back to the lawyer's call. Why leave money to the dead? Who was the beneficiary?

{

Leda called Himmel's German Language Bookstore in York-ville, New York's native German neighborhood, but they'd been of little help and sniffy about her request for any book they had on Nazi Germany that contained references to homosexuals.

"As Madame might understand, we carry few books on that period and certainly none on *that* subject. The period is not popular with our customers. I can't help but agree with them that it's best forgotten. Raking up all that awfulness, and for what?" Mr. Himmel asked.

"So we won't forget and let those bastards get up to their ugly business again," she answered and slammed down the receiver.

Then, as she hadn't since she was very young, she swore at length in gutter German. I'm getting nasty, she thought, and then, Well, why not? If you can't let people know what you really feel when you're about to kick off, when can you?

She called a friend at the New York Public Library who was helping her place her private papers with a university. Could he get someone to go through the library's collection of books on Nazi Germany and find any that contained references to homosexuals? She'd pay the person or make a donation to the library for their time. She also wanted a list of the best books on Nazi Germany through 1936, if there were such things, as well as a list of the best general histories.

As she had often played benefit concerts for the library and been personally generous, the list came three days later. Her friend at the library called to be sure she'd gotten it.

"Will you please thank whoever put the list together," Leda said.

"Of course. I'm also calling to ask a question. I hope I'm not out of line, but the researcher wanted to know why you were interested in homosexuals in that era. She could only find four references in the indexes of the three hundred or so books she checked. She's an expert on the era and she says they're rarely mentioned because they're only marginally important in the history of the period. You've piqued her curiosity."

"You must tell the woman that she is remarkably wrong. They were very important to the period, because Hitler hated them enough to try to destroy all of them. Tell her that the story going around Berlin at the time was that Hitler hated them because he had to work as a *Lustknaben* during Germany's Depression. Have you ever seen pictures of him as a young man? He was a rather handsome young monster."

"Lust-what?"

"*Lustknaben.* I've heard the American word for it. Give me a moment. Oh, yes, the American slang is 'male hustler.'"

"That's impossible."

"Why in the world would you think that?"

≀

She called Scribners' and a week later sent Maria to pick up forty-three books.

"Five dollars I had to give the cab driver to bring in the bags, Madame," Maria said. "After the extravagance of what he charged to ride in his filthy cab. So awful. Cabs used to be clean, and the drivers knew where they were going. Remember those wonderful hatches in the top so you could see the sky and buildings, and the jump seats, and they would get out and open doors, help with packages? Hah!"

"Put the bags on the bed, Maria, and go get us some coffee. Bring two cups, Maria. I'd like you to stay and give me a hand unpacking the books and sorting them. Hand me one of the bags."

Maria brought a bag to the bed and said, "Always in such a hurry over everything, Madame. You should conserve your strength."

Leda said, "I've got a deadline," and began to laugh. "I usually hate puns, Maria, but I like that one."

"Madame must not make terrible puns like that. It hurts me to hear."

"I apologize, Maria. It was thoughtless. I forget that other people's feelings can be more tender than mine. I've had to be strong for so long, face so many facts, that it's hard for me to be otherwise. Bear with me. But I know you do. You always have."

"I love you, Madame. What do you think my life will be like without you? Over thirty years with you. You and Paul are my family."

"Give me a hug, Maria. But not too hard."

Maria gathered Leda to her and thought of birds with their hollow bones.

"Now, go get us that coffee, Maria. And Oreo cookies. Bring the whole bag. The hell with my diet."

}

Leda sorted the books by topic and lay back, wondering where to begin her journey to a past she had fled only steps ahead of the police.

The covers of most of the books were remarkably similar: funereal black with pseudo-Germanic typefaces and an ominous swastika that now screamed of atrocities. Hard to believe she had once regarded the swastika as an abstract symbol of a political party when she had first seen it in her hometown of Herne. It hadn't yet become the century's Mark of Cain.

Then the Nazis captured the government and their symbol was everywhere. It was emblazoned on the ubiquitous posters that pictured radiantly healthy blond *Volk* — the common people elevated to racially pure heroic status — or stern strong men carrying wrenches or pitchforks or guns. The symbol was on stamps and money, the labels in clothes, in the background of movies, on buttons, even bread wrappers. She remembered the hundreds of Nazi flags lining Berlin's Unter den Linden and hearing their racket when they snapped like whips in the wind.

She took a book from the top of a pile and read: *Nazi Culture*. "That's a laugh," she said and dropped it to the floor. She picked up a small red book. *Missing from the Holocaust: Forgotten Nazi Victims,* by C.R. Doyle. She opened the thin, ill-made book and read the table of contents, found a chapter that interested her, and began to read:

DESIGNING THE PINK TRIANGLE

The pink triangles sewn on the breasts and legs of prison uniforms to mark homosexuals in the Nazi concentration camps were in the making long before they appeared; some Nazi bureaucrat merely symbolized long-nourished hatred. These pink markers were only three and a half inches across, but they were as deadly to those who wore them as bullets.

Anti-gay attitudes were made law in nineteenth-century Germany when Paragraph 175 of their criminal code outlawed homosexuality. Until the Nazis seized power, it was rarely useful or expedient to enforce the law, but it did prove sometimes useful politically to accumulate official dossiers on those who were gay.

By and large, Germany seemed to care so little about whether someone was gay that, in the Nineteen Twenties, Berlin became an international mecca for gays, with an atmosphere so free of prejudice that the gay Magnus Hirschfeld established his Institute of Sexual Science there to undertake the first serious research in human sexuality. The atmosphere was so welcoming to innovation that, in that decade, Germany, and especially Berlin, produced world-class painters, musicians, composers, movie makers, architects, and performers who startled and enriched the world.

This richness of the arts and sciences was in stark contrast to the nation's bottomless poverty. Hordes of children walked city streets to beg, steal, or prostitute themselves, and were often a family's only source of income. Families of six could barely afford the one room they lived in and hunger was an unremarkable commonplace. The once-powerful German currency traded at four trillion marks to a single American dollar. Government was immobilized and useless.

One of the nation's few hopes was Hitler's National Socialist Party, the Nazis, with its militaristic enforcement arm, called interchangeably the S.A. or the Brown Shirts, that trampled everyone who resisted the movement's march to power. Hitler's S.A. was under the direction of his closest friend and champion, Ernst Roehm, a man who was as gay as he was ruthless and the one responsible for getting his rich gay friends to provide major funding for the Nazis. Roehm's closest aides and advisors were gay and the S.A. attracted and welcomed large numbers of disenfranchised and poor gays to their ranks. The Nazis offered hope, comradery, great potential for political power, and one badly needed free meal a day. By 1932 the Brown Shirts numbered 400,000. Roehm also controlled the Hitler Youth movement for children that was the breeding ground for the next generation of Brown Shirts. The Hitler Youth motto was, "Out of the Hitler Youth an S.A. man will emerge." The motto caused a certain amount of rude laughter, but there was no humor in Hitler's cry for "vigorous, commanding and cruel young men with the strength and beauty of young beasts of prey," and that is what Roehm supplied plentifully. A majority of Germans came to believe that the Nazis did have a "solution" to the nation's killing ills, and were too poor and oppressed to look ahead to the time when the solution would metastasize into the "final solution." Hitler plowed fertile ground.

What had Roehm looked like? Leda wondered. She flipped to the illustrations and found his picture. His face was almost as broad as it was high, and his expression was wary. Maybe he didn't like having his picture taken. She could see why: He was ominously gross. He wouldn't just eat, she thought, he'd devour.

Roehm wore a uniform rich in braid. His temples were shaved and his hair was a slicked-down patch over his high forehead. Wide-set eyes, a small, finely drawn nose, and a taut line of mouth under an uncertainly sketched mustache completed the face, except for a deep scar the caption said was from a bullet. The scar zagged down his nose, across his right cheek, and then continued down his jaw. A formidable face. Hard to imagine him in fond embrace with one of the young blond Nazi "gods" he was said to favor. He was so dangerously unlike the gay men she had known in Berlin and since. So disturbingly unlike her beloved Dieter.

She went back to her reading:

Thanks mostly to Roehm, Hitler became Germany's chancellor in 1933, using a calculated mix of murder, assassination, arson, and intimidation to do so. It was only when Hitler stood near the apex of power that he deemed his old comrade Roehm and his thuggish Brown Shirts a dangerous embarrassment. Besides, Hitler wanted to cut a deal with the army, who saw the Brown Shirts as a challenge to their own power. During secret negotiations, the army told Hitler that their price for their allegiance to him was Roehm's head. Hitler went to his task with lethal enthusiasm, because he, too, had come to fear Roehm's power and popularity.

Hitler set the stage for gay persecution in 1933. The first book burnings and anti-gay demonstrations had taken place when Storm Troopers, accompanied by a marching band, stormed the Hirschfeld Institute, savaged the building, and destroyed its library, all to the accompaniment of martial airs by the band. To further ignite anti-gay feeling, the burning of the Reichstag, Germany's "Capitol Hill," was blamed by the Nazis on a homosexual, although it was agreed unanimously that the arson had been ordered personally by Hitler.

The start of the "Blood Purge" or "Night of the Long Knives" took place in the very early hours of June 30, 1934, and began with the murder of two S.A. officers at the Ministry of the Interior in Berlin. Hitler was present and said, as he kicked one of the dead bodies, "These men were not the most guilty," likely thinking of Roehm who would live a few more hours, till Hitler's henchmen could reach him at the Hotel Hanselbauer in Bad Wiessee, where Roehm had gone for a short holiday.

Many stories told of that day are contradictory, a muddle of "official statement" and rumor. One often told is that Roehm was found in bed with a handsome S.A. lover and both were dragged out of the hotel and shot, as were many other S.A. men, there and elsewhere, gay or not. Officially, only a few dozen people were said to have been killed to suppress a "homosexual plot." Very likely, hundreds — more likely thousands — were murdered, a mix of S.A. men and those Hitler deemed dangerous political enemies. The jolt of terror this sent through Germany discouraged questions.

Hitler presented this purge in terms he knew the German people would believe, even welcome, respect, and applaud: He informed the masses that, thanks to his prudent and swift amputation of this ulcerating limb, Germany was made safe from the spreading homosexual cancer. Now, German youth was safer, the state more secure, and, most important, the good and pure German *Volk* were cleansed of a stain no good German could bear without soul-destroying shame. Hitler wanted the German people to feel proud of his actions, and a vast number did. There would be no more of the despicable *Vergnügungswut,* the madness for pleasure that had been rotting the reawakening will of the Aryan people. The tone of Hitler's radio address on all this was sorrowfully celebratory and Hitler was cheered by the press and public. Hitler had ascended a mountain of corpses to get to the heights of popular power. The criminals would now write the laws and Hitler guessed rightly that he could exercise any tyranny with the sanction of wholesome popular sentiment.

But there was to be no overt witch-hunt in the S.A., for Hitler knew that, even with Roehm dead, they remained a popular and powerful force. Instead, he would splinter them over time. With that policy, Hitler rendered the remaining gays in the S.A. schizophrenic, as they would now embody both victims and victimizers.

What Hitler set out to do, and accomplished, was to create a culture dense with self-deception, while he himself governed without illusions. He gave the people a vision of a land full of genetically manipulated blue-eyed blonds who were all of one mind. He taught them to deal with the world, not as it was, but as it might be, if they could just get rid of those who didn't fit or insisted on being different.

Capitalizing on the pervasive anti-gay anger he had so successfully orchestrated, Hitler broadened Paragraph 175, with additional homosexual crimes spelled out in Paragraph 175A that extended gay "criminality" to include touching, kisses, and glances and, later, would add Amendment A, making any real or imagined homosexual act punishable by death. Brutal enforcement would be managed by the S.D. Section II-S for the "Control of Homosexuality," but that came later, as did a law and enforcement agency that commingled the crimes of homosexuality and abortion under the Reichs-Center for the Fight against Homosexuality and Abortion. From 1933 to 1945, anti-gay laws were under constant revision to make them an ever-wider, ever-finer net.

Gays were among the first to be herded into the new concentration camps that sprang up in 1935 – Sachsenhausen, Natzweiler, Fühlsbüttel, and eight others – and were among the first to die in them, as they were also among the last dying in them in 1945, being singled out for the most draconian punishments these Hells could devise. Gays were used in experimental medical operations, without anesthetic, deemed by doctors as essential to the war effort. Gays were given assignments to work details known for their low survival rate, murdered by their overseers when they were no longer wanted for sex, and simply murdered for amusement or out of pique. Other gays died the way most camp inmates did, of hunger, exposure, disease, beatings, and commonplace mistreatment.

Paragraph 175 and 175A remained law until June 1969, as the conquering Allied armies seemed to feel it was too embarrassing to deal with gays as victims of the Nazis. So, those gays who did elude their "emancipators" were, if caught, reimprisoned to serve the sentences not satisfied by their time in the concentration camps. Thus, many gays who were fortunate enough to elude their rescuers remained liable for their crimes and unserved sentences until Paragraph 175 was repealed twenty-four years after the end of the war.

Researchers of that period and of the Holocaust have been reticent in dealing with the "delicate" subject of homosexuals, but recent scholarship puts the number of gays who died under the Nazis in the many tens of thousands.

The pink triangle and the horrors it symbolized were not, as the Nazis claimed, a spontaneous expression of "offended national sensibilities," but the culmination of orchestrated prejudice to serve political ends. Hatred of gays was elevated to a place alongside patriotism, duty, and virtue, and too often remains so.

Leda closed the book as old sorrow and rage swept through her.

}

The next morning Leda awoke feeling wonderful, except for the nagging sense that something was wrong. It took her a long moment to realize that what was missing was pain and the confusing effects of drugs.

She slipped out of bed, a little unsteady, but markedly surer on her feet. She tried to rise on her toes, but quickly realized that was overdoing things.

She was briefly elated and longed to delude herself that a miracle had occurred. She knew better. She recognized the "false spring" of the gravely ill that was both a blessing and a warning. Well, if she'd been given a respite she would use it and enjoy it.

She slipped into her red silk robe and was astounded at how large it felt. The belt could have gone around her twice.

The first thing she wanted was a face. Not just lipstick, but a full makeup. She had missed the morning ritual of lipstick and base and blush.

It was barely light when she slipped upstairs and sat at her dressing table with its array of makeup. She held out her hand to check its steadiness and began. She took her time, enjoying the effect, making alterations to accommodate the hollowed cheeks. Finally, the face she hadn't seen in months emerged and she was enjoying looking at her handiwork when Maria rushed into the room, saw Leda at her dressing table, and burst into tears.

"Oh, Madame, you disappeared. I've never been so frightened. You mustn't scare me like that. I've been running all over."

"I didn't mean to frighten you. I'm sorry."

Leda turned and smiled brightly.

"Madame looks wonderful. But you mustn't scare me. I brought your breakfast and..."

"No soft-boiled eggs this morning, Maria. I'm going to come down to the kitchen and you're going to make me French toast and bacon. And fried pineapple slices, if you have any."

"Does Madame think that's sensible?"

"Madame's starved."

Leda ate with zest and Maria beamed with pleasure to see Leda's appetite returned, even dared to imagine Madame gaining weight.

Leda was on her third cup of coffee when Paul came hurrying into the kitchen. When he saw Leda he skidded to a halt and tried not to look surprised. He sat at the table and said, "Something smells wonderful. I'll have the same, Maria."

Maria was delighted. How long had it been since she'd seen her family at the kitchen table?

It was a joy for the three of them to pretend. Paul tried not to fret about Leda not taking her medicine, but couldn't bring himself to spoil the illusion they were sharing.

"Do you know what I'd like to do today?" Leda asked. "I'd like to go to Lutece and have a nice three-hour lunch, but before anyone tells me I'm nuts, I know that's out of the question. So, I'll settle for lunch in the garden. Crabmeat salad with lots of mayonnaise and that lovely Soave we brought back from Italy last year. And if there's nothing pressing at the office, Paul, I'd like you to stay home with me."

"I can't think of anything I'd enjoy more." Then, finally unable to curb his concern, he asked, "Would you like me to get your medicine?"

"I don't need it, Paul. Isn't that amazing? And I'd like a clear head. Taking that stuff is like dropping a veil over the world. I feel fine."

The neglected garden had gotten a little scruffy and sooty, but it was a wonder for Leda to be in it, finally outside. She decided she would dress beautifully, even put on jewelry. It was a warm August day, but Leda gave in to Maria's insistence that she have a light cover for her legs. Leda resisted, until she was outside and realized how little she could feel the August heat.

The lunch was over and cleared, and Leda and Paul sat lingering over the wine.

Leda said, "What I'd like more than anything is to never have to go back into that sickroom, Paul. Being outside is such a small thing to feel so extraordinary."

Paul put his hand over hers and stroked it gently. "More wine?" he asked.

"Oh, no. I can feel it. I want to be clearheaded. There's something you should know. Knowing Prescott, he called you about my curious request."

"Yes."

"I've never said much about my life in Germany, because there was a lot about it I wanted to forget. But now it comes back all the time. That's what all those books are for. But all they've told me is how accurately I remember that dreadful time.

"There's all this talk about the mind burying truly awful events. It doesn't. They stay and they're vivid, and they don't lose any of their potency.

"I have never lied to you, but I've begun to think that my silence has amounted to one. I've been reticent about a couple of men I knew in Germany. Important and lovely men.

"Before you get the idea your old mother was a loose woman, let me say I had only one affair when I was a girl. You shocked?"

"Should I be?"

"Just a little, so I can remember I was once young and irresponsible. But Rudy disappeared. Then Dieter. Both vanished.

"I'm getting ahead of myself." She pushed her wineglass away.

"Let me start over. You see, I've gotten it into my head that he may still be alive. Facts — all those books — say that's not likely, that he's probably long dead, but I can't stand the idea that if he is alive he may need help.

"That's why I want to set the money aside in my will."

She knew she still wasn't being clear and shook her head, as if to shake her thoughts into order.

"I'm going the long way round, Paul, because I'm a coward. All I should do is tell you the lot and hope you'll understand."

"Are you asking me to forgive one lover? You couldn't do anything I wouldn't forgive."

Considering what needed to be forgiven, she hoped so.

Chapter 2

For the first time in her life Leda felt like a grown woman as she strode along the platform beside the hissing train that would take her home to Herne. She reveled in the weight of the broad-shouldered tweed coat she wore thrown casually over her shoulders and didn't care that it was open to the wintry chill in the station. She delighted in the tingle of cold silk on her legs and rejoiced in her aching calves and pinched toes, because they were the discomforts of her first pair of high heels. Mama had sent her off to Berlin a good young girl and here, two days later, she was striding confidently through Berlin's vast Potsdamer railway station, her head high and topped by a frivolous mite of a velvet hat hairpinned tightly to her newly marcelled hair.

Leda's porter looked at the ticket she gave him, bowed courteously, and strode off with her parcel, pausing to be sure she followed, before he entered the second-class coach of the *Essen Express*. She had seen movie heroines board trains and they always did it so beautifully, smiling down on a lover and looking longingly at him as tears glinted with the aid of artful lighting. She looked back down the platform, smiled poignantly at the world at large, and disappeared into the coach. Music up, fade out.

Halfway down the corridor the porter waited. She tugged off a glove and tipped him too much with a coin damp from her tight nervous grip. He gave another little bow and she nodded gravely.

Her mother told her that the midafternoon train would be best, because there would be fewer people and fewer of the Brown Shirts, or SS, who now seemed to be everywhere: "I don't want you speaking to those men. Don't be rude, but those kind of men often can't tell the difference between a respectable young woman and ... well ... other kinds."

"But Willy's a Brown Shirt," Leda argued.

"Willy's an exception. We know his family and we know his intentions toward you are honorable. And you have been raised to be respectable," her mother said in a tone that closed argument.

Leda prayed she didn't look nearly as respectable as she had two days before.

Oh, God, how she wanted to be flirted with. Nobody had flirted with her on the way to Berlin. Who would? Her mother had dressed her in a blue jumper and sailor hat, sensible brown walking shoes and brown cotton stockings. She had been put on the train to Berlin looking exactly like what she was, a Lutheran minister's daughter.

Good heavens! Going for an interview at the world-famous Hochschule für Musik dressed like a girl in the chorus of *The Prince of Pilsner*. She was the pianist who would dazzle the world: Wasn't her scholarship both an acknowledgment of talent and a promise of greater achievement to come? Dear God, she certainly hoped so.

In only two days Leda had, as she thought of it, "emerged." Of course Mama wouldn't get to see the new Leda, the transformed woman who had known the fleshpots of Berlin, and gotten daringly tipsy on beer with raspberry syrup. Berlin had been magic. Rudy and Dieter had been wonderful. She could have wept as the train began to move. She didn't want to go home ... ever.

{

Rudy Mueller, a student, had been sent by the school to meet her at the railway station and given money for a taxi and a miserly tip. He toyed with the idea of taking her by trolley, but if she was important enough to warrant special treatment, that might be unwise.

In the taxi on the way to the school, Rudy said, "You're a surprise. I've heard you play on the radio and my teacher speaks of you with great admiration. I was expecting someone much older. You play so maturely. I would have missed you, if you hadn't come up to me."

She flushed and fought tears, and looked down at her plain sturdy brown shoes as if they had died on her feet.

"I know just the thing for you," he went on. "I'll take you and my little sister to lunch tomorrow at the zoo. You two will have a lot to talk about."

"How old is she?"

"Twelve."

Her tears poured.

Rudy had no idea what had caused the outburst and, as he would with his little sister, he put his arms around her and pulled her to him, murmuring, "There, there. Nobody will hurt you. It's a big city, but no one would dream of harming a pretty little girl like you."

"*Whaaaaaa!*"

"I've said the wrong thing."

"I'm seventeen."

He was wise enough at twenty not to say, "I don't believe it." Instead he said, "Look, we don't have to be at the school for another hour. How would you like coffee at a smart cafe? Of course, we'll have to take a trolley from there."

She blotted at her tears with one of her father's huge white handkerchiefs and nodded rapidly, brightening.

The coffee and the torte were splendid and she tried to remember not to eat too fast and embarrass herself. She was always hungry. She scrubbed her lips with her napkin and then her grief spilled out: "I can't stand what I look like. I read every issue of *Jungselle* at Sophie's, so I know what's in fashion. Mama says good girls — even girls who play with symphony orchestras — don't dress like Marlene Dietrich. Especially a minister's daughter. Even the long gown I have for concerts makes me look like an old pillow. Mama says, how would it look in Herne for me to be showing off in city clothes; people would say I was getting above myself, that I was proud.

"Well, I *am* proud. I've played in public for seven years, since I was ten. But I live in Herne and when I come home from performing, it's back to school and housework and music lessons in Essen twice a week and evenings with Sophie or Willy, and awful school uniforms."

As she babbled on, Rudy smiled at her benignly. She recognized that smile; older people gave it to children, along with a pat on the head. He did think she was like his little sister. No one saw her as a woman.

She sighed at the sadness of it all and continued to spill out her many sad concerns: "It's getting worse since those Nazis got into office. I have to take time from practice to go marching like a goose with those BDL girls and pretend I believe all that nonsense about having lots of babies for the Fatherland. Inga is only sixteen and big as a house with a baby she got at a Hitler Youth rally in Weimar, and her mother could shoot that Hitler."

Rudy glanced about nervously to see who was sitting nearby and said in a voice just loud enough to be heard at nearly tables, "The Nazis will give us a most glorious future, even more splendid than our present."

Leda looked puzzled but sensed his wary uneasiness.

He took her hand, leaned toward her, and whispered, "It doesn't do to criticize the Nazis in public."

She didn't understand, but nodded anyway.

"You need some help, Leda. Can you stay over?"

"Oh, no. I mean, Mama would ... Why?"

"I have a student friend who works as a model at Wertheim's. She is very chic. She could help you pick out some clothes, find you a hairdresser, maybe even get you a discount."

She felt a thrill go through her. Pages of *Jungeselle* flipped through her mind and she saw herself in all those wonderful clothes she longed for in that magazine, saw herself standing tall and poised in high heels, looking twenty, even twenty-one, as old as Rudy.

"But I couldn't go home like that. And they'll all be at the station to meet me. I can't get off the train looking like *that.*"

"Like what?"

"A ... a Berlin woman."

"We'll work that out. Do you have any money?"

"I ... I ..." She couldn't say it. She did have money and she had brought it all with her. Had she been planning to do something wrong? Was her mother right, would money lead her to sinful vain ways? And, God forgive her, it was money she had stolen. She hadn't meant to, but when she had been invited to play at a Nazi gathering in Dortmund they had given her her usual fee and she had hidden it, telling her mother that the Nazis had paid no fees this time and said that the honor of playing for Party leaders and for the *Volk* was sufficient reward. Her mother had looked sour, said that was just about what one would expect of that lot, and believed her. Leda had what seemed a fortune.

"Yes, I have money," she said and thought, God, help me and, Mama, forgive me. I'm going to do something awful. At last!

Magic was happening. Magic had already happened: Here she was at the Cafe Kranzler on the Kürfurstendamm with all of Berlin parading past. In some wonderful way all she surveyed was hers and she knew the day would come when people would walk by, notice her, and whisper to one another: "Isn't that...? I do believe that's *Leda Kohl!*"

A knife-edged screech shot through the air, making the people in the cafe duck their heads and many press their hands against their ears, looks of pain contorting their faces. Leda was staring anxiously about, her mouth open, an expression of shocked fright making her eyes look immense. Rudy took her hand in both of his and tried to look reassuring, saying, "It's nothing. It's just speakers."

Leda's expression shifted abruptly from fright to puzzlement. "Speakers?"

Rudy nodded toward a tree at the curb where a truck stood. A workman in dark coveralls was emerging from the thick leaves down a ladder, saying something over his shoulder to the man who steadied the ladder.

"Loudspeakers," Rudy said. "They're putting loudspeakers in the trees on the Kürfurstendamm. They're just testing them."

Leda still looked puzzled.

"For public announcements," Rudy explained. "Herr Hitler likes to ride down this street. It's nice and wide, so there's room for the crowds. These loudspeakers will tell people when he's coming and play music as he passes in his car. You'll see. He stands in his open car and salutes, and the people go mad with excitement. I've seen him; he always looks stern and loving, like a good German papa. The papers say the speakers will also be used to warn us of enemy activities."

"What enemies does Germany have?"

Rudy leaned close to Leda and said softly, "The Nazis will undoubtedly let us know."

Leda sat stiffly on the uncomfortable oak chair in the director's outer office watching his secretary shuffle agitatedly through immense heaps of paper that were piled on every surface. The woman frowned, mumbled something that sounded like a curse, shook her head, and went, *"Ach! Ach! Ach!"* reminding Leda of one of her teachers when she got completely out of sorts.

The director had sent his compliments and apologies to Leda for being late for their appointment, explaining that these days it was hard to keep to any firm schedule. On this day more Nazi authorities from the bewildering array of new councils and committees had come unannounced to check again on the Jews or Communists or whatever other undesirables might have slipped through their ever-finer screening process. Matters at the school were changing so rapidly that it was almost impossible for the secretary to know who was in school, who could be in school, who must go into the army, or who must be reported on regularly to the Nazis. Miss Braemer knew little of music, but loved the students and took pride in being associated with a world-famous school. It distressed her to see them sorted by alliances, rather than by talent. Miss Braemer stole glances at Leda and didn't like what she saw, which was a perfect little *Bund Deutscher Mädel,* one of those vapidly pure Aryan maidens so prized by the Nazis – a hick's daughter who just happened to have a small but undoubtedly "genetically unsullied" talent. And now this girl was to come to the school with Nazi endorsement, while others with great talent were hounded out.

No auditions for this one, no applications, just one letter from some Nazi bigwig and in she came. These days they were getting nothing but the Nazi's pets.

Miss Braemer was at the boil when she snapped at Leda, "I hope you know what a lucky girl you are. Do you? Did you know that Gruppenführer Stoll has personally arranged for you to be exempted from all admission requirements? Not even any obligatory State duties for you. You must have a lot of influence where it counts."

Leda pressed back into the hard chair, caught off guard and frightened by the angry scorn she heard in Miss Braemer's edgy voice. "I met General Stoll at a concert. He was very nice to me and said he would write you. My parents have never..."

"And you come at just the right time. Our enrollment is down, way down. You will receive so much extra attention, now that there are so many fewer students. After all, why waste our time teaching Jews or other undesirables? They can do so much more for the Fatherland digging ditches, don't you agree? Do you know what I'm looking for in this mess? I'm hunting for undesirables and I never know from week to week who's going to be undesirable. They send me lists of names, or new guidelines for detecting those who are unworthy of the State's support. And I empty the drawers and sift through the files and report what I find. And then the students are taken away or never come back. But you don't have to worry about any of that. You're one of the chosen. And I don't give a damn if you tell them what I've said. All these poor talented children being punished to make way for the likes of your kind."

Miss Braemer slammed back her chair and started from the room, colliding with the director as he entered. She slid past him and ran as he watched. He knew she was running to her daily sob in the bathroom, and he wondered what had caused today's eruption. He looked at the distressed girl in his office and hoped Miss Braemer hadn't said anything impolitic to this young woman who came cloaked in such powerful protection.

He made an extra effort to sound welcoming and cheery: "You must be Miss Kohl. Sorry to keep you waiting, but I had a meeting about teaching staff."

He noticed the effect that Miss Braemer had had on Leda and said, "We're badly overworked these days and poor

Lotte's mother has been very ill. We must make allowances, mustn't we?" He wanted to add: "It's hard purifying ourselves to suit the Nazis. We're losing our best teachers and students." But the young woman before him looked the healthy embodiment of German stock, and bigger men than he had been brought down by indiscretions spoken in front of children.

As he took Leda on a tour of the school, he spoke as he knew he should, extolling the work the school was now doing – under the guidance of the new regime, of course – in bringing a purified musical culture to the students who would go on to spread its glories to the beloved people, the masses of *Volk* who made up the soul of their nation.

What else could he do? The new leaders had already named the men who would be able to fill his position admirably, should he feel unable to "execute vigorously" the new aims of the State.

They wound through the vast old brick-and-iron building. Leda said little to the people she met, for there was music everywhere in the building; soprano overlapping cello, piano colliding with oboe, and yet there was no discord in the sounds, except for the jarring counterpoint of the director's vigorous advocacy of purified German music. What was the director trying to tell her? Why had Miss Braemer been so cruel about ... about what?

They ended the tour back at his office door. He didn't ask her in, as he wasn't sure what state Miss Braemer would be in, and he was not anxious to remind her of Miss Braemer's possible indiscretions. "We'll do our best for you, my dear," he said, "and that can be considerable. I know from what I've heard of your work that you will be a credit to us. That's why we're willing to forego all the usual admission requirements."

Leda wondered at his courtliness. Why so deferential to a student? Leda didn't understand that Stoll's letter of recommendation had been taken as an order from a powerful Nazi, which is exactly what Stoll had intended. "Would you please tell Miss Braemer that I hope she's feeling better and that if I did anything to offend her, I'm sorry."

Now the director was puzzled, but somewhat relieved. "Your mother's note said I should try to let you get away by four so you could get a train that wouldn't get you home too late. You're sure you can get to the station by yourself?"

She was both offended and depressed by his condescension, but answered, "Yes, sir. And thank you. I can't tell you how much I want to do well, how hard I'll work."

She thanked him several times before she hurried off, not starting to run till she was out of his sight, then tearing down the two flights and out to where Rudy had said he would wait.

They planned their strategy over sandwiches. Leda would call Mrs. Muntz, who had the only telephone near her home. She would tell her mother that the director had been called out of town and that she had to stay over to see him the next day. Her mother would carry on, but what could she do? Tell her to come right home, that's what. A suitable lie was needed. *No, Mama, the director's secretary is taking me home with her for the night and will give me dinner. Yes, I'll get the two-twenty train tomorrow.*

Leda called her mother and, amazingly, she grudgingly agreed that Leda could stay in Berlin overnight. Rudy was magic; he did work wonders in her life. Now she would ask for one more bit of wizardry. "Pleeeeease," she wheedled in a tone that always worked with Willy, "I don't want you to think I'm awful or not well brought up, but it's just that ... *wellll* ... I would very much like to see ... *wellll* ... I'd like to see something I shouldn't see. Oh, Rudy, please take me to some perfectly awful place I shouldn't even know anything about."

Rudy laughed. She was very much like his little sister. "I could get into bad trouble taking you to some dreadful place, especially some of the ones I know." It was a slight boast.

"Everybody wants to protect me. Why is that? Do I look so fragile? I've played concerts all over the country. I've met generals. I've even met their mistresses. I know I'm not supposed to know about such things, but I seem to know a lot I shouldn't. I just never get to see it. How am I supposed to learn about the world? I thought you were..." Oh, what was that word Louise Brooks used so much? "...cosmopolitan!"

Rudy was stung, his urbanity questioned, and by someone barely more than a child. Well, if she wanted decadence, he would just have to figure out where. He was less informed about depravity than he cared to admit, even to himself, and his hand in his pocket fingering coins told him how meager his resources were. But he was damned if he was going to lose face. Besides, he had credentials as a man of the world, so he would just have to think of someplace special, someplace memorable, and someplace cheap. And he thought he knew just where. If only Dieter were playing tonight, he might be able to take her to the Blue Wink, and wouldn't that impress her? If Dieter could arrange it for free, that is, and if Dieter were still on good terms with the maitre d' now that their affair was over. So, he might be able to produce an elegant evening of modest depravity for no more than a few tips. He called Dieter and explained his problem.

"Still wasting your time with women?" Dieter teased.

"That's your fault, Dieter. I love you, but you have all the wrong bits and pieces."

"My bits and pieces have made me very popular in certain circles. But if you won't have me as I am, I suppose you may as well bring along your latest woman."

"This one's not even a woman. I mean she's just a girl who's going to be attending the Hochschule. I got stuck with her and I've got myself into something of a corner and..."

"Well, come along. I'll set it up with Magnus. Just sign the check when they bring it and I'll see it's taken care of.

God, but it will be good to see you. I've missed you."

"I've missed you, too. And it's wrong. Friends shouldn't have to..."

"Shhhh!" Dieter hissed at him and said, "Maybe it won't be for much longer."

Rudy cooled a little and said, "See you later. You're a good friend."

Rudy next materialized a room for Leda with a woman student, then summoned up his model-friend from Wertheim's to find her some clothes in which she might pass as an older woman, and got another friend to mask Leda's freshly glowing face under a coat of makeup.

Leda considered her artificially matured image in the mirror and was thrilled not to recognize herself. For the first time in her life she wore a dress that showed she had breasts, and she marveled at how the makeup made her look faintly world-weary, even a little cheap. Wonderful! Nothing of Herne showed through. And best of all, she was going to see the depravity that was gossiped of in Herne when good people whispered of that depraved "sink of sin," Berlin.

⟨

Actually, Berlin's sinful reputation was suffering stunning blows. Within weeks of coming to power in 1933, Hitler's new regime had purified Berlin's notorious nightlife of places like the Trocadero, a bar renowned for the most brilliantly deceptive drag in a city renowned for female impersonation. Voyeurs were deprived of the city's favorite sideshow at Berlin's Mikado on Krausenstrasse, where gays of every stripe used to mingle in a giddy democracy of proclivities. Gone, too, were the Adonis Diele, where very young men sought "fathers," and the Schnurrbart Diele, which catered to those with a fetish for large and baroque mustaches and who approached one another teasingly stroking their mustaches while challenging, "Mine is bigger than yours." Missed, too, were the Nüremberger and Kantdiele, where conservative middle-class burghers found compliant young male companions. Perhaps the greatest loss was the Silhouette, the most elegant in decor and clientele, where the evening's scene had the glamour of richly gowned and jeweled women and glossily affluent men that von Stroheim and Lubitsch had put on film to shocking effect for the awed and envying masses.

The Nazis had closed all gay bars, except for those owned or frequented by powerful Party members. Also open were those designated as places where the authorities could keep track of vulnerable gays foolish enough to remain public. These later bars were officially proclaimed "degenerate" bars and included places like Ferdy's, a *Danzbar* where gays compliantly herded themselves to dance and be monitored. Because Ferdy's charged more to cover what they told customers were "additional official expenses," patrons wrongly assumed the extra charge bought them protection. There was no protection from the watchers.

The bars that were officially permitted were no longer exuberant places, but possessed a furtively subdued air. The glances that now shot toward new arrivals as they entered were anxious rather than expectant. Patrons no longer looked warmly at an opening door in the hope of seeing Adonis, but peered anxiously in the hope it wasn't the authorities.

The official – and publicly applauded – Nazi line on all this was that the State had become a "hothouse of sexual imagery and stimulation, smothering sound Aryan impulses in the suffocating perfume of modern eroticism" and that this stench must be cleared from the Aryan air, so German nostrils could fill again with the fresh clean air of a purified nation. Of course, such absolute purity was for the betterment of the masses; the powerful might do as they wished.

The Berlin Leda so guiltily itched to see was mostly gone. Of the bars that straddled the line between straight and gay, the Blue Wink was one of the more successful, being neither officially sanctioned nor deplored.

The Blue Wink was a Hollywood fantasy of blue mirrors, chromium, and glass partitions etched with fanciful swans and ladies draped in carelessly placed yards of gauzy fabric. Immense white plaster whorls swept intricately from floor to ceiling and all was black and white, as was the Norma Shearer movie that had inspired the Hungarian Jew who originally owned the club and who had created the elaborate interior. The club rose in three tiers from a white marble dance floor, so that the entrance on the top tier afforded an elegant panorama. The Blue Wink boasted a splendid trio for dancing and, popular in his own right, Rudy's good friend Dieter Holtman, who played between the trio's sets.

Only one change had been made by the Nazis: the Hungarian Jew was gone. The new owners were an experienced manager and two wives of highly placed SS men who had acquired the Blue Wink with a small amount of money and large threats that had pushed the owner across the Atlantic to safe poverty in New York City. The women were lovers, as were their husbands. With such well-placed sponsorship, the gaiety for which Berlin was famous had not been entirely subdued at the Blue Wink, merely moderated into something less riotously obvious. The transvestites were more maidenly, the gay men more reticent of gesture, and the *Lustknaben,* the gays for hire, of the best class.

Rudy was gratified to see how awed Leda was by the place. It was a very quiet night, and thanks to Dieter's prompting Rudy was given the ego-building welcome of a regular by the maitre d' and led to one of the best tables in the ring that circled the dance floor and commanded a view of the bar and its exotic denizens.

Much to the waiter's amusement Leda ordered beer with raspberry syrup, one of the few exotic drinks she had ever heard of, and Rudy retained his man-of-the-world status by ordering a gin martini with an olive.

The trio was playing, but only two couples languidly circled the small floor, more in touch with one another than with the music.

Leda looked around casually but, not finding what she had come to see, began to peer about intently. It was all so sedate. No one danced on tables or wore glittering evening dress or kissed and writhed in corners. Necklines didn't plunge, men didn't stroke sinisterly thin mustaches. There were no phones on the tables for calling from table to table, from handsome stranger to ravishing femme fatale. Where was the sinning? Had Rudy tricked her and taken her to a perfectly respectable nightclub? If this was a terrible place to be, she wanted to know why. Sounding faintly aggrieved, she asked Rudy and he smiled and told her to look around.

Because her knowledge of sin was limited to sneaking off to movies like *The Blue Angel* and *Lulu* after music lessons in Essen, she wasn't sure what she should be looking for. She shrugged and said, "I don't see anything. Most of them look bored."

"A lot of them are."

"My father always makes sin sound so interesting. And it's wonderful in the movies." Had she said that? She moved her drink away.

"I'm afraid you're too late for the best sinning. That was last year," Rudy said. Then, having second thoughts, added, "No. Actually, we are officially ordered to be sinless. But there's a little left."

"Are you teasing?"

"No, just being slightly ironic." He smiled to underscore that he hadn't meant to be condescending and looked around to see what she might find shocking.

"You see those women on the far side of the bar? Well, they are known as 'ladies of the evening.' The expensive species. For a price, those men you see talking to them can go to bed with them.

"You see the three women at the other end of the bar? They are not women. They are men who like to think of themselves as women and, usually but not always, like to sleep with what they call 'real men.'"

"They're not women?" Leda asked, staring. "But they're wonderful. They look so assured, almost more like women than women."

Rudy said, "But they're not supposed to. What if some good German man mistook them for real women?"

"That would be very funny."

"Don't you know that good girls are supposed to be shocked by such things?"

"Oh, good girls. I know I'm supposed to be shocked, because it's expected. But what's shocking about it?"

He'd make one more try, he thought, saying, "And the other men at the bar are *Strichjungen, Lustknaben,* whatever you want to call them."

"Which is...?"

"Berlin slang."

"For?"

"Men who are available for a price."

"For work, you mean."

"Of a sort." He smiled.

"You're laughing at me."

"No. It's just ... delicate. They're male whores."

She looked toward where the men stood and considered, before she said, "It must be a hard thing to do. To give everything you are to someone just because they have money."

Then she fixed Rudy with serious attention and said, "I keep feeling you're laughing at me when I don't know something you do. You shouldn't. How could I know? It's just that I haven't seen much of the world. But I intend to. So, please, don't laugh at me."

He was startled into silence and the best he could manage was a surprised nod. Other girls he'd brought to places like this did the expected and gasped in shock. Leda merely saw and assessed.

Still, Rudy was a little disappointed at her calm acceptance, while she felt cheated. She'd been sure from all she'd heard that there was a lot more to sin, that people would look feverish and hectic, the music would be raucous, and the dancers riotously abandoned, not like these couples moping about the floor. Sin should be stimulating and abandoned, and it wasn't. It didn't seem all that interesting. People sipped their drinks and spoke softly, the trio's music was mostly romantic, and the laughter merely amused. She again had the traitorous idea that maybe her father was wrong about sin.

She said, "There's no magic in sin, is there?" and Rudy felt he had somehow failed her.

He finished his drink and hoped the maitre d's indulgence would extend to another. He signaled to the waiter, who quickly returned with another round.

The trio's set ended. As their pianist slipped off the bench, Dieter slid on and provided a seamless change for the dancers. Dieter smiled toward Leda and Rudy and made a palm-up gesture to them to get up and dance.

"Would you like to dance?" Rudy asked.

"I can't, yet."

"I could show you."

"When I come back," she said, expressing an assumption he welcomed. She listened with obvious pleasure as Dieter segued from song to song, most of which were unfamiliar to her.

She gazed at Dieter and said, "He's wonderful. Your friend plays beautifully."

"He was one of the school's best students."

"He graduated?"

"No. Thrown out. Just like that. Overnight."

"Why?"

"I think he should tell you, if he wants to. But he may not want to, so please..."

She made a slight gesture that dismissed the idea that she might pry, and said, "He's so handsome and he plays so wonderfully that I like him already. You like him very much, don't you?"

"He was my best friend at school. I miss him very much."

"Don't you still see him?"

"Not as often as I'd like. We're a little dangerous for one another."

"Friends aren't dangerous. That's silly."

"Don't call things silly you don't understand," he snapped and she shot back, "Then tell me what you mean. Don't just call me silly," but quickly added, "If you can't tell me, just say so."

"It's not a secret I should have to keep, so why not?" he said and immediately thought of any number of reasons not to tell her: talking so unguardedly to a young girl sponsored at the school by the Nazi party, taking her to a place like this, pointing out people and things the Party had criminalized. But he was tired of cutting his thoughts to fit the national model and whittling his feelings down to such a small, but acceptable, size. He knew it might be dangerously foolish, but he spoke, his tone slipping along the edge of belligerence: "I'm what's called a *Mischling,* a part Jew. It's a small part – a great-grandmother – but enough Jew to make me non-Aryan, unfit for this new order. They say that my sort shouldn't even have children. I've been declared unwelcome in my own country."

His voice was now harsh and, like the school director's secretary, he seemed to be accusing her of terrible offenses she couldn't identify, much less defend.

"And Dieter is worse off. I probably shouldn't tell you, but he's a homosexual. He's undermining the will of the people to multiply, to make more pure-blooded Aryans, more good, right-thinking people who are all of one narrow mind. Just think how awful he is. Dieter can't or won't sleep with women and make babies, so what the hell good is the little faggot to the Fatherland? Jews are dangerous. So are faggots. We've become dangerous to one another."

"I'm sorry."

"Damned right! But there it is, and I miss him very much."

Leda had a surprising thought and her question was out before she could censor it: "Were you and Dieter very special friends?"

Rudy looked blank and Leda pressed on, "Like the men at the bar."

Rudy laughed. "No. I have my girlfriends and he gets involved with the damnedest lot of no-goods he can find."

"Talking about me again," Dieter said, surprising them by seeming to materialize. Dieter made an exaggerated bow and then went on, "Too true. Terrible sense about men and I make no babies for the Führer. Well, let him make his own babies."

He pulled out a chair and sat, as Leda said, "But he's much too old."

"He only forty-six," Dieter said and Leda asked, "Isn't that too old?"

Rudy said, "You must beware of the gray-haired, miss. Hasn't your mother told you about all this?"

"She tries, but she just ends up crying."

Dieter said, "Then I'll tell you all about it."

Rudy scoffed, "And what do *you* know about it?" but Leda took Dieter's hand and asked, "Would you? I don't just mean about ... what? ... the different parts, but all sorts of other things."

Rudy looked away and Dieter said, "We're embarrassing him."

"Well, it's not the place," Rudy sulked.

"Where better? That's what this place is all about. And look who's worrying about Leda's virtue. She's just arrived in Berlin and you're plying her with liquor and introducing her to lowlifes like me." He turned to Leda and added, "But my life's not nearly as low as I would like it to be."

He laughed and said, "Here I am, telling you all about myself and we haven't even been introduced. You must be Leda Kohl and my name's Dieter Holtman. Rudy says you're going to the Hochschule. Wonderful place. I envy you."

"And you should still be there," Rudy interrupted.

"Don't be angry for me, Rudy." Then, to Leda, "He's a very political man. You should have heard him go on about Hindemith when the school chucked the man out. Days and days of Hindemith. He doesn't like his music, but Rudy loves a principle."

Rudy began to feel uneasy about all they were saying so candidly to this girl and decided to change the subject when Leda asked Dieter, "Do you play here every night? You play so much music I've never heard. What was that song with the funny choppy rhythm?" she asked and dah-dahed the complex melody line with remarkable accuracy.

"'Fascinatin' Rhythm,'" Dieter answered. "It's American. Gershwin. I can sing it phonetically in English, but I've no idea what it means. I like it because it's like a little dynamo, and I can barely sit still when I play it."

"Where can I buy it?"

He told her about the last shop left permitted to sell American sheet music and then where the best-stocked music shops were in Berlin, and what recordings there were of Gershwin's works and where. And Dieter and Leda were off in a rush of talk about the songs he had just played and who had composed them and who sang them best and why they were banned as degenerate and never played on the radio. Rudy made no effort to interrupt, and only felt slightly put out that Dieter was monopolizing his date. Well, not really a date. Just a new acquaintance.

Leda liked Dieter. She liked anyone who understood music, not as simply notation that could be produced on an instrument, but as an intimate conversation between player and hearer, the player saying, "Let me help you hear what I hear, feel what I feel." She liked listening to Dieter's voice and the offbeat stresses he gave words, as if there were a melody line in what he was saying, and she felt proud to be treated as an equal. In her enthusiasm she said, "Rudy said that you're not studying, and you should. You really should. Why not some other school? Or you could teach or give concerts. You're really wonderful."

Leda was sure she had seen a look of acute pain cross Dieter's face, but it had been so quick and the smile that came was so bright, she thought she must have been wrong. He smiled charmingly as he said, "I'm something of a man without a country these days. I disgraced the school, to say nothing of all of Germany. It's why they threw me out of school. I would never have left. I loved it there, but I had to make a living to go there, so I worked as a female impersonator at the Lorelei."

Dieter could see her puzzlement, so he explained, "I dressed as Ginger Rogers and danced to 'The Carioca' with a cardboard Fred Astaire. Acres of black ostrich feathers. I also did a passable Ruby Keeler. Sewed all my own costumes. Down to the last sequin." He held up his hands for inspection. "Clever hands. But it's not as if I enjoyed it. Drag doesn't really interest me, but the pay was very good."

"Drag?" Leda asked.

"Men dressing as women."

"But why?"

"It's amusing." Leda's expression said she still didn't see, so Dieter added, "It's unexpected, out of the ordinary, and people find it funny. It turns sex upside down. Anyway, after that terrible Roehm business, the club was raided and we were all hauled off to jail. I could barely get all my taffeta into that tiny black police van.

"It's a shame they didn't arrest the customers too, but then who would be left to run the army? My fingerprints were taken with some awful greasy black stuff it took me two days to get off. I was released and the school was told to get rid of me. 'But he's good,' the school said. 'But he's bad,' the police said."

"That's terrible," Leda said.

"That's modern life," Dieter answered.

"Why don't you study somewhere else?"

"I'm on a list somewhere under the heading 'Silly Fairies Who Must Not Be Allowed to Study Music.'"

"Leave the country."

"I can't. People with arrest records can't get passports. I even work here under another name, or the club would get in trouble. All in all, I'm lucky not to be locked up."

"That's not fair. Just for dressing up as a woman. I'm sure you were very good."

"Sadly, that's true and that's what made it all the worse."

"The law is silly."

"Oh, no. You see, I did it in public, on a stage, and corrupted the military. What if a soldier gets so confused he can't tell a man from a woman? Think what it would do to morale. Rudy, you must educate this young woman in modern German thought, before she gets herself in trouble." Then, to Rudy, "Before you get yourself into trouble."

The bantering tone was suddenly gone and Dieter looked at Leda intently and asked, "Should I be telling you all this? You see, people like me don't know who's safe to talk to anymore. It's nothing personal. It's just hard to know who to trust."

"You mean I shouldn't tell anyone what you've said."

"Never."

Leda sensed that a profound shift had suddenly taken place in the conversation and that something grave, some commitment was being asked of her. She had made promises to keep secrets as a child, to eat dirt or kiss a toad if she told. She sensed this was not a promise that, if broken, her mother could pat away or kiss better. This promise would be of a remarkably different order and, she sensed, would have to be based on understanding the many meanings under the words. But she didn't understand all that had been said. How could being a little Jewish or a homosexual be so dangerous? Still, whether she fully understood or not, they deserved her commitment to respect their secret.

Rudy and Dieter were becoming uncomfortable with her silence, fearing it might mean they had gone too far with the wrong person. She saw their disquiet and said, "Of course I won't say anything. I just don't see the wrong in what either of you have done, but you have my word. Of course you do."

The relief she saw on their faces told her how important her word was. She also knew that she had just done something very adult, and that the trust she felt in their looks was a weighty obligation. She felt very close to them and grateful to them for treating her as an intimate, even an equal. All of them sensed that something grave had passed among them and they began to like one another very much.

Being uncomfortable with so much seriousness, Dieter said, "And to show my appreciation, if you ever need a gown, let me make it for you. I could give you a very good price."

"Oh, could you? I would love a decent dress for concerts."

"Not 'decent' at all, my dear young woman. And not in the least discreet. Something seductive that will give you center stage, that will eclipse an entire symphony orchestra. I see you in Nile green watered silk ... yards of it. And no jewelry, except for stunning diamond earrings. I have just the pair. And I'll show you how to make an entrance in it, how to listen for that moment of silence before your entrance and catch it ... then dazzle them with a head-up sweep onto the stage. How to let them know they're in for something breathtaking."

Dieter stopped and cocked his head toward the bandstand. "They're almost done, so I have to get back. What would you two like me to play for you?"

"More of that American music," Leda said. "You choose."

"Something romantic, to suit your debut in Berlin with one of its handsomest men."

Rudy shot him an irritated look.

"I have just the thing," Dieter said. "A beautiful little Kern tune called 'They Didn't Believe Me.'" He hummed a bit. "You see, I only play the American Jews – Kern, Dietz and Schwartz, Berlin, Arlen. I do it as my political protest. It cheers me up to think of all these good Germans seducing one another while under the spell of Jewish music."

Dieter gave Leda a small bow and said, "It was a great pleasure meeting you. When you come back I'll loan you some of my music."

"And the dress?"

"Watered Nile green silk," he said and was quickly off, just regaining the piano bench as the trio's last note died, and immediately launching into the Kern piece.

"He's wonderful, isn't he?" Leda said.

"He plays extraordinarily well."

"Oh, yes, the music too. But I meant him. Something very special in him."

"I don't know how he's stood up to all he's had to deal with and stayed ... what? What describes it? Happy? Good-natured? It's something more, but I don't have a word for it."

"He suits himself."

"Yes. Still Dieter."

"Is he really in danger?"

"Yes," Rudy answered. "And things just get worse. I wish I knew how to get him out of Germany."

Rudy looked toward Dieter with a helpless anxiety and Leda said, "Oh, Rudy, I think you should help me, because I don't understand all you've been saying. Miss Braemer was furious with me, I made you angry, Dieter's in danger. I don't know what it's all about and I don't know what it has to do with me, but I suppose it does somehow, and it scares me."

He reached over and took her hand, saying, "Maybe it's just the raspberry beer. As for me, it's the martinis. They always make me gloomy. Would you like to dance?"

"I really can't."

"Neither can I."

They rose and moved to the dance floor, as Dieter watched and segued into the song that was the current favorite of his newest lover. Brand-new. By Harold Arlen.

"Fun to be fooled.
Fun to pretend
This little dream won't end."

The next afternoon a smartly dressed young woman walked toward Rudy outside Wertheim's department store, gathering assurance as she approached and delighted by the effect she was having on him. She almost laughed at his look of pleased surprise.

He smiled. "Extraordinary, madam. Delightful, madam. Come along, madam, Berlin should see you."

They walked down the Unter den Linden toward the Adlon Hotel and she took pleasure in his sidelong glances. It was exciting to be noticed by a man. She knew that Willy at home no longer saw her; she was just there, the way a sister would be or, for that matter, a bathtub. Her mother said that

Willy's familiarity was to be expected after years of growing up together, yet she still noticed Willy, marked the changes in him and, though hard for her to admit, didn't like them, liked him less all the time. Well, the devil with Willy; she was in Berlin with an attractive man, the day was lovely, and Willy could stay where she'd left him in Herne.

Rudy talked of the school and the teachers: who was good, who was crotchety, who superb but difficult, what to expect and not expect, whom to turn to in trouble, whom not to confide in. "And I'll be there if you need help. The school wants you. You're a prize, Leda, and they know it. You already have a reputation. They know you'll get better and they'll share the credit."

They found a cafe he knew he could afford on Behren Strasse. He was running late and had to gulp his coffee. He rose and stood staring down at her. He could barely believe this was the same girl he had met only yesterday. He hated to leave her, but he had a class in composition, and discipline and promptness at the school was essential. More importantly, he was at pains not to call attention to himself.

"I don't want to go, but I have to," he said. "You have two hours before your train. Will you be all right? Is there anything you need? You're sure you have your ticket and money for the cab?"

"Yes, Papa."

He laughed and started away, then came back, bent over and kissed her on her cheek, knocking her hat askew. It was done clumsily, but they were both pleased.

He started away again, but stopped to call back, "I'll remember to ask about a room where I live. Good-bye. Safe journey. I'll write. You be sure and write."

Of course she would. He started away again and she called, "Thank you, Rudy, and give my love to Dieter." He turned and she could see he wanted to come back, but she waved him away with a gesture that told him to hurry. He broke into a run.

She bought a map at a kiosk and strolled the beautiful avenues of one of the world's most cosmopolitan cities, her Wertheim's box with her little-girl costume tucked under her arm. Wouldn't the men who gave her admiring glances be surprised at what was in that box? Was it really this easy to go from childhood to being a woman? Well, with her very own Merlin, why not?

As she stood before the Imperial Palace she was struck by a sense of the rightness of what was happening. It felt right, as Herne never had. There was room enough for her in Berlin, space in which her spirit could range. The streets were full of people who looked interesting, as if each were worth knowing, and she was sure they all did fascinating things. The air was rich with promised spring, but it was also laden with her future, with music, with endless possibilities, even immortality.

⁊

She sat contentedly watching the countryside sweep past the train window. She caught flashing glimpses of farmers at work, their wives and children often by their side in the fields. She noticed the army transports that seemed to be more and more in evidence. She marked the red, white, and black flags with the swastikas atop every train station and the posters on the station platforms that spoke of the *Volk* and their place in Germany's new order. She'd heard it all, of how society was being reformed to serve the people and of how they, the newly exalted *Volk,* would be shaped to serve a purely Aryan society. Join this, support that, don't tolerate this, give your all, and we'll all be as one in a single superior race, in one nation that we will create in our purified and purged image. Leda cared for none of that. What did it have to do with her?

They were nearing Essen, but she was loath to go into the ladies' room and change back into the clothes she'd left home in.

She checked her new clothes in a locker in the Essen train station and hung the key alongside the gold cross on the chain around her neck. She felt awkward and constrained, itchy and shamefully childish in her old clothes.

As her train pulled into Herne she saw her parents waiting on the platform, along with her brother Karl, Willy, and her best friend Sophie. They looked somehow different, but this was not a new feeling for her, nor was the sense that they were something of an embarrassment. She knew she was part of them in some unalterable way, but she knew she was different, almost alien, and, now after Berlin, even more so. She wanted extraordinary things from life, but had learned early that if she spoke of these wants, all she did was upset people. Her friend Sophie could not conjure a world beyond Herne and her family; Leda could not imagine a future among those she loved.

They stood in a row waiting for her, as if they were posing for a picture, and their expressions offered welcome and love and safety. She knew they were eager for her news and, for her sake, wanted it to be wonderful. It was, but that would make them sad and her ecstatic. Why wasn't home enough?

Her father wore his clerical suit and, as always these days, Willy was in his Brown Shirt uniform with the short pants. Sophie wore her new dirndl and her blonde hair in braids. Leda's brother imitated their father's dark clothing and serious mien.

Leda hugged her mother and kissed her brother and father on the cheek. Willy winked at her over Sophie's shoulder as Sophie engulfed her in large soft arms. She was home and she knew what the rest of the day would be like, what all the days remaining in Herne would be: they would be what they had always been, what they must always be if she stayed. But she wasn't staying. She couldn't.

≀

Still wearing his Brown Shirt uniform, Willy called for her at five-thirty. Her parents approved of him and made no secret of their expectation that they would marry. Willy treated her as if she were already his, as if it required no effort on his part to have her, and she resented it.

They walked toward the city's town hall, where the advertised "cultural event" of the evening was "As I See Siam," an illustrated lecture by Nazi-appointed Cultural Director Rucke's cousin. Leda said, "Why don't we just go for a walk or go sit in the square?" She wanted to ask him to take her for a beer with raspberry syrup, but knew better. He would say that only men should drink, that drinking cheapened women. He tightened his grip on her waist and she could feel the sweat from his palm seeping through. He said, "It is my duty to attend Party-sponsored functions. They'd notice if I weren't there."

She felt rebellious. He didn't care what *she* wanted, didn't take her needs into account, because he felt they were irrelevant. She knew he thought of her music as a suitable amusement for a child, to be enjoyed before the more serious matters of being a wife and mother must be undertaken, but of no substance in the real world.

Under the weight of her painful thoughts, she moaned, and Willy stopped and turned her toward him. "What's the matter?"

"What?"

"You moaned."

She seized the chance and improvised, "I knew I shouldn't have eaten the pork. It always does this to me. Too much pork and I'm in agony. I really should go home, before I embarrass us."

"You're a foolish girl. If you know pork upsets you, why do you eat too much? Now look what you've done. You've wasted the ticket and I shall have to sit alone. If we run, I can get you home and still get back in time."

"I can't run. My stomach hurts." Then, fearing she might be overdoing matters, she said, "But I'll be all right if I go slowly. I've had this before. You go on. You must be there. It's your duty."

"I must tell your mother to make you be careful with what you eat. I told her she shouldn't let you go to Berlin alone and I'm right. Staying overnight in that city. To study for what? You should learn a few lullabies for our babies. You don't always have the best sense. You must learn to be a responsible woman."

"You go ahead or you'll be late."

"I'll come by later," he said.

"I'm going right to bed."

"I'll come later and visit with your parents."

"Oh," she said as she stood and watched him march off. He marched everywhere since first putting on that damned uniform.

{

His uniform was a year old. Leda had first thought of it as a quirky joke, but the joke had gone on too long and there was no more fun in it, certainly no fun to be made of it, because Willy took it very seriously.

The first night he had worn it was the night the Browns — those who wore the brown shirts of the National Socialist party — had marched through Herne, announcing their allegiance to the newly elected Nazi party. Exactly a year before, they had paraded on orders from the Party and had heartened, awed, dismayed, or frightened those who watched. Men of all ages had strutted militantly with loaded guns through Herne's tranquil streets to converge on the city's district office. Their orders were to take command of the district office, city hall and other public buildings, and to raise the Nazi flag above each. It was happening simultaneously all over Germany that night, in towns of all sizes. It had been ordered to be done without warning, at one surprise stroke.

The trouble was that full-sized Nazi flags had not been provided, only handkerchief-sized ones were to be had, so these were raised and these scraps of flag flapped foolishly and barely visible above imposing ornate stone buildings.

Word of the march had spread quickly, and Leda had rushed with her parents and brother as if to a circus. Distractions were welcome and well attended in depression-poor Herne.

Leda had been surprised by the men in the marching columns. The Brown Shirts had been around long before Hitler's ascension to chancellor in January, but few respectable people would have anything to do with them; they were usually Herne's lags and bullies, with a smattering of World War I veterans, the "old fighters." Leda knew almost all the men marching − her mother's butcher, her father's sexton, several of her teachers, members of her father's choir and flock, even some of the town's wealthy, all recent recruits who scented the wind's direction. And, of course, Willy marched. It was too dark to see how well they marched, and one could barely see the black-and-red swastika armbands they wore. Several times the marchers tried to sing the "Horst Wessel" song, but hardly anyone knew the words. For all the strutting and "Seig Heils!" the event seemed ragged and overblown, like an amateur production of *The Student Prince*.

Leda and Sophie got grudging permission from their parents to go to the town square, and there they saw Willy and his school friend Kurt standing at attention outside the city hall, rifles at their sides, cigarettes hanging from their mouths.

She thought Willy looked even younger than usual when he played soldier, his ineptness with the cigarette accentuating the effect. Leda whispered to Sophie she was going to go up to Willy and tease him, but Sophie sensed his seriousness and told Leda she shouldn't. Sophie perceived the grim reality behind what Leda saw as foolish theatricality.

That night Leda spoke to her father about the parade and what she thought was just a lot of pompous showing off. Why all those awful guns? Was this some kind of army?

"No," her father answered, "but they are all Party members now. The Party is for the poor man, my dear. There's much about the Nazis I don't approve of, but I don't like unemployment and hunger either. They make promises like all politicians, but they seem to get things done. You know how hard it's been for us, and we've been lucky, much better off than most. Such awful poverty leads to many terrible sins. Maybe the Nazis can help us regain our self-respect." He thought of the many women he knew whom hard times had pressed to prostitution, of his parishioners who had committed suicide, but he said nothing of them to Leda. "If they can give people bread and hope, maybe they are what we've been praying for. All that marching around was just a gesture, just something to tell people things are starting to happen. I pray God they're going to get better. Somebody has to do something."

The next morning Leda's father visited two parishioners in the hospital, members of the anti-Nazi parties. One man was a Black-White-Red, the other a Black. Both had been severely beaten by the Brown Shirts. Pastor Kohl temporized with them, suggesting that the violence was only a passing aberration and that things would quiet down now. That afternoon he soothed and counseled a local official who had not only been forcibly evicted from his office, but also compelled to sign an agreement never to run for office again. The day brought other news of beatings and harassment, and of others driven from public offices already refilled by Nazis. All this in quiet little Herne where almost nothing ever happened.

His sermon the following Sunday was shaped to solace the troubled, but not provoke the victors. He spoke of the ever-difficult choice between bread and freedom and discoursed on what the Scriptures meant when they advised that men did not live by bread alone. But his message became muddled as he tried to reconcile bread and bloodletting. Leda didn't pay much attention, because she was going to play a new Bach piece for the recessional and only hoped that if the Nazis helped the town recover there would be some money to repair the church's ailing organ.

≀

"Of course Willy believed me about the pork, Sophie," Leda explained. "If I get found out, I'll say I came here because I felt too ill to make it home. If Willy asks — which he won't — you just tell him I was terribly sick and you even had to hold my head when I threw up." Leda looked over Sophie's shoulder into the mirror and asked, "Do you like the color? Isn't it daring?"

Sophie was feeling wonderfully wicked as she inexpertly applied the Jazz Girl Crimson lipstick Leda had brought her from Berlin. It was against all the rules in Sophie's life — against school, church, home, and Party — but it was deliciously adult.

"Oh, Leda, it's just the best gift I've ever had. What a wonderful color. It's so depraved." She spun around, striking the provocative pose she'd seen a temptress strike in a movie when challenging her lover to kiss her. Sophie pursed her lips and purred, "Well, Count Rudolph, are you a man or not?"

She and Leda fell into one another's arms in a cascade of giggles.

"Where did you ever find it?"

"Wertheim's."

"Oh, how gorgeous. You were in Wertheim's?"

Leda gave Sophie a luridly colored account of her time in Berlin, of the Blue Wink, of the daring women and men and those who were both, of riotous drinking and of her dancing with an older man of twenty, almost twenty-one. And as Leda talked, Sophie felt the familiar ache of jealousy that Leda's stories of her adventures always evoked and which always made her feel guilty about envying her best friend. This time it was different; this time Sophie's pain welled up into tears.

"Oh, Sophie, what's the matter?"

"Me. *I'm* the matter. And it will get worse, because you'll be gone in a few weeks. Oh, Leda, what's the matter with me? I'm not anything you are. You have talent and you're small and pretty and you're going to Berlin and you've already been out with an older man."

Sophie sat on the edge of her bed, making no effort to blot the tears streaming down her face as she spoke. Leda went to Sophie's dresser, picked up a handkerchief, and sat next to her friend, dabbing at Sophie's cheeks as she hugged her. Sophie was so deep in her accumulated sorrows that she hardly noticed.

"I'll barely earn my school certificate, Leda. I'm not even smart. That terrible Hilda screams at me at the BDL meetings that I'm too fat and I don't march right and I drag down the others and ruin all she's trying to do to make us strong German women. She's right. I am too fat and I have a face like the bottom of a frying pan. You're pretty and talented and you go everywhere and meet everyone, and you're going away to be famous. And I'll miss you and don't know what I'll do without you."

Leda felt her friend's pain and was surprised. It hadn't occurred to her that her leaving would cause this much hurt.

"But you're good, Sophie. I'm not good, not like you. And I'd like to be sometimes. I'm a bad daughter. I accept money from my parents that they can't afford for my lessons. I've even stolen. That's how I bought those clothes. And what's worse, stealing it didn't bother me. I feel wicked, because I know I'll go to Berlin and be so happy I'll barely miss them. All I seem to really care about is me and it makes me feel unnatural, and I watch you and wish I were like you. You love people the way my parents do. You'll be a wonderful wife and love your children. I don't even want a husband or a baby."

Leda surprised Sophie, who stopped crying abruptly. "But you'll come home when you're done. You're going to marry Willy."

"He hasn't asked. Everyone just assumes. He's laid out the rest of my life without even asking me. When he's eighteen next month he can apply for the SS, but first he has to do Labor Service and two years in the army, and then the SS will *consider* him. Then he'll *consider* me, if my grandparents prove genetically pure. And he'll put me somewhere to have his babies while he goes off and plays soldier. I'm no better than one of his damned chickens to him. And I don't want it. He says Germany doesn't need more musicians, it needs more good mothers. Everyone just moves me about without my having any say. Oh, Sophie, how do I stop it?"

Sophie had never seen Leda in pain and she forgot her own and put her arms around Leda, who sat staring within herself, looking for something she couldn't find.

"I think I'll miss you more than anyone, Sophie."

"We'll write every day."

"Yes, and you'll come to visit."

They sat hugging one another as they often had throughout their short lives when a parent had been unjust or their report cards proclaimed their shortcomings or when life seemed too much to endure. But as Leda hugged Sophie she tried to imagine her friend in Berlin and knew with painful certainty that Sophie wouldn't fit. Leda hated herself for that knowledge.

She stayed too late at Sophie's and was hurrying through the dark familiar streets barely noticing how little she could see. She was happy Sophie had liked the lipstick so much. They had always loved being naughty together, and the courage either lacked they were able to give one another for...

The slap came out of the dark with such surprising ferocity that it tore Leda's breath from her and she tottered in terrified silence back against a building. For the first time in her life she felt the breathtaking numbness of fear.

"You will never lie to me again. Never! I will not have a liar for a wife."

Oh God, it was Willy.

"You may do what you want with your parents, because they think you are their little angel, but you will tell me the truth. I will not permit this kind of behavior, just because you think you are this famous pianist."

What was he talking about? Her wits were coming back and she felt the heat of anger rising like a fever. What was he saying? Telling her what she could and couldn't do, what *he* would permit, what *he* would tolerate? How *dare* he! Without thought, she began to raise her hand to strike him when she became aware that they were not alone. Across the way, barely visible, stood Willy's newest friend, his Hitler Youth leader, Jurgen. She could just make him out, but an ugly smile of approval for the scene Willy was staging for his benefit gleamed maliciously. She forced her hand back to her side, willed it quiet, because she knew that if she hit Willy in front of this man, he would be obliged to strike back.

The air between Willy and her was heavy with the reek of beer. She mastered her fear, but she knew she must be cautious with Willy, mustn't stir him to prove his manly pride in being a bully.

"Oh, Willy, it was not a lie," she managed. "I hurt too much to get home and I was sure I was going to be sick to my stomach in the street. I just couldn't stand the idea of ... of people watching. I barely made it to Sophie's. Just ask her."

She improvised and hated him for making her lie, but lies were all he deserved ... and evasions and disdain. But now she must placate him, be frail and frightened. "I'd never do anything to hurt or upset you. Why would I do that?"

She talked on, earnestly and soothingly, careful to be still, trying hard to be believed. Her vision was now clearer and she could see him fairly well and see that he was totteringly, disgustingly drunk.

To the inebriated Willy her voice seemed satisfyingly humble and contrite, and he was happy for Jurgen to see him assert himself. Jurgen was right: A man had to make the rules at the start or lose control, and what kind of man was it that could be run by any woman. They were the kind of men others laughed at, that's what. The kind who had no future among the strong. He owed it to Leda to be the kind of man other men admired. Jurgen had read these remarkable truths to him from the paper when they were at the inn. Goebbels had written, "The mission of women is to be beautiful and to bring children into the world. The female bird pretties herself for her mate and hatches the eggs for him. In exchange her mate takes care of gathering the food and stands guard and wards off the enemy." He must be stern and not allow lies, must not allow Leda to think she could do as she pleased. She would do what he, her superior guardian, wanted. And he would put his foot down on this Berlin nonsense. Why go, when she must only return to bear his children?

He became blearily aware that she was walking away. Oh, yes, she had said she would obey. And, yes, her walk, like her voice, seemed slow and humble. Yes, he should let her go home alone. Going with her would be a sign of weakness, would lose him the advantage of his newly asserted power. She turned the corner and was gone.

"That's the way," Jurgen said, dropping his arm over Willy's shoulder. "If you don't set her right now, you'll lose your balls and be a pussy."

As she walked her breath came back and her fear was replaced by cold rage. How dare he? As if she was his chattel. You will never bully me again, Willy, even if I end up bloody on the street. And you would beat me, because that's what you're learning, that's what you're being taught by those heroes of yours. Damn you!

In a terrible way the slap propelled her forward, even farther out of childhood. She saw how her relationship to Willy was a child's assumption carried into the present. It didn't have to be this way. It wouldn't be. No one would ever shame her like that again or make her that afraid. My God! Marry that fool?

She reached home, but didn't go in. She wanted time alone and the minute she walked into the house she knew she would be a daughter again, because that's all she knew how to be among these people. She had felt like a different person in Berlin, like someone who had choices. She understood that all that could save her lay in the future, and the future and Berlin were one.

{

It was a brilliant June morning and the train to Essen stood ready and growling impatiently. Leda faced her family and Willy and Sophie, just as she had when she had come home two months ago. Her mother wept and her father gripped her mother's shoulder. He knew better than to tell his wife she shouldn't cry when her only daughter was going off to a city whose reputation for moral dangers was a worldwide scandal. Leda's brother had startled her that morning with his hug and by bringing her magazines and her favorite chocolates and saying, very uncustomarily, that he would miss her and pray for her safety and success. Sophie's tear-streaked face was buried in Willy's shoulder. Willy was looking soldierly and controlled and disapproving, and he stood patting the weeping Sophie perfunctorily.

Was this how she would remember them? Would they be forever assembled in her mind, caught in sorrowful tableau at a train station? She wanted to look sad for them, to match their misery at parting. She hoped she looked a little anguished and that her sense of relief at finally being off didn't show too clearly. She prayed to a God she rarely thought of, "Don't let me hurt them. Give me a little sadness at leaving, because I know they care. Don't let them see how happy I am."

⸮

"I sometimes think my poor parents gave birth to a changeling. They were good people and they made great sacrifices for me, but your uncle was truly their child. Not just looks, but if you want to see your grandfather, just look at Karly. The best I've ever been able to hope is that I made them proud."

"But you saw them again."

"Only that once, that last Christmas, and I was hell to be around, because I wanted to be in Berlin. I broke off with Willy that visit and added to the uproar. Willy said it was their duty to God and the Nazi party to beat me until I came to my senses.

"I fled back to Berlin, and all the way I prayed I'd never see Herne again. That taught me to beware of praying, because I got what I wanted. I never went back home. All hell had broken loose in Berlin and, as things turned out, I ended up having to flee the country. At first, I didn't go back to Germany because the authorities were after me and I didn't know where I stood. Then the war came and, after it was over, I couldn't bear to go and see what had happened to

−70−

Germany or meet people I felt had brought it on themselves.

"I didn't even know my parents had been killed by a bomb until after the war ended. I only found out then, because I was able to pull some strings through friends in Washington to get Karly back there.

"How awful for Mama and Papa. All alone, their daughter a wanted criminal. I learned my letters home were intercepted, so we became lost to one another.

"All such old stuff, but here it is again, alive and well, and awful as ever."

"What in the world did you do? Is that why you never talk about that time?"

"No. Actually, once I escaped and was safe, I was rather proud of being a criminal, considering my crimes. All that bothered me was that my crimes didn't work."

She sipped her coffee, said, "It's cold," and was putting it down as Maria hurried into the garden and over to Paul, whispering, "It's Mrs. Howe. She wants to see you."

Paul made a face and asked, "Did you tell her I was here?"

Maria nodded, and Paul sighed resignedly and rose.

"I suppose I must."

"You didn't forget her allowance?" Leda asked.

"She calls three days before it's due to remind me."

"An efficient woman. If she's here to pick over the goodies, say I'll be happy to leave her anything she wants. She's been after those huge Chinese vases for years. Ugly things. Tell her to take them with her. Why wait?"

"They're too big to carry."

"Knowing her, she'd strap them to her back, like a coolie."

"I'm not angry with her, Mother. Why are you?"

"General principles. Go intercept her, before she comes out here. Say I'm asleep and not available for viewing."

Paul disappeared into the house.

Maria asked, "Should I bring more coffee?"

"Wait till Paul comes back."

"Don't let the woman upset you, Madame."

"She's picked a rotten time to run out on him. And not even for another man. She says she's going to 'find herself.' God help her if she does. She'll find a vapid nonentity. My problem with her is that she's too good to stand. Always so reasonable and tasteful. In almost twenty years I've never seen her do or say one wrong thing, never heard her excited or unreasonable. What galls me most is that she calls me 'Mother Howe' and I've never been able to get her to stop. Why did Paul pick her?"

"Oh, I think she picked him, Madame."

"He didn't have to go along with the gag."

"She was the most beautiful woman of her season."

"What you're saying is that Paul mistook good bone structure for character."

"I'll go start the coffee."

"I must be feeling better, Maria. I'm being bitchy. It feels good. Come sit down and gossip with me, Maria."

Paul returned to find the two women sleeping in the drowsy light. It saddened Paul to see that even with her artful makeup, his mother looked as old as Maria.

He went into the house and wandered aimlessly from room to room looking for a mystery novel he'd been reading, still living in the atmosphere of his mother's story.

When his mother asked about what his wife had wanted he would lie. He would tell Leda that she had come out of solicitousness, but his mother had been right, her real purpose was to conduct a covert inventory. It was already agreed by their lawyers that she would get the two-bedroom apartment on Sutton Place and the place was already chockablock with furniture and knickknacks and souvenirs of her crafts courses. What Paul found odd and rather funny was that she seemed to covet pieces his mother hated; he knew it would give Leda gleefully perverse pleasure to be sure she was willed the lot.

In that moment Paul realized how little he felt for the woman he was divorcing. No, not "little" — nothing. Could almost twenty years leave so small a residue? He found he could barely resent her.

He awoke from his self-absorption to find himself on the third floor. He went into the bedroom that had been his as a child and where he'd taken to retreating to read his mysteries and think. He sat in the window seat that looked down into the garden and wondered where his mother's tale was leading.

Hardly anything out of the ordinary in what she'd told him so far, except for her unexplained "crimes." And she'd sounded so casual about them that it was difficult to imagine they could amount to much. As she'd said, "Such old stuff."

What most fascinated him was that these were the first glimpses he'd ever had into a time she had never spoken of more than glancingly.

His own past was very much on his mind these days; if he couldn't look forward to life without Leda, he had more than enough time for looking back, and was surprised to find how little there was to see. He told himself ruefully that he could write his autobiography on the head of a pin. He certainly hadn't lived the life he was raised to. His growing up was full of interesting places and people. Then he turned eighteen and Leda started urging him from the nest. He'd postponed college for navy service, thinking he might follow in his father's footsteps, make the navy his career. But after life with Leda, the navy felt rigid and he disliked having decisions made for him. He'd then done two years of college without finding direction or a consuming interest. When his mother's manager died, he'd taken over the office for a few months, met his wife-to-be, married, and just continued to run his mother's concert and recording affairs.

That's the lot, he thought, and the pin isn't half-full. How had he settled for drift? At first life with his wife was a pleasant change from running around the world with Leda. Their life was a ritual of well-mannered parties, peopled with his wife's dignified friends, undemanding work, demure tidy sex, and topical impersonal chat over meals. He'd never even thought of divorce or a mistress when his wife crossed her legs permanently three years before. His life had the excitement and dash of a Brooks Brothers catalogue.

In his more honest moments, Paul thought, "My wife doesn't bore me, I do."

He knew he needed a future but, for now, he could only live in the limbo of Leda's slowly passing present.

His only excitement came from mystery novels that he consumed indiscriminately, barely caring about whodunit.

≀

Leda awoke with a start. She was alone. The remains of lunch had been cleared. Someone had draped a stole across the top of the chair and down over her shoulders. It was still warm, but she didn't feel it.

From his third-floor window Paul saw his mother stir, clutch at the cover on her legs, then pitch forward onto the slate paving.

≀

The doctor said, "Mostly bruises from the fall, but your mother's stabilized and we can probably release her tomorrow morning."

"She was more like her old self today than she's been in months. No pain, good appetite."

"In any major illness, every so often there are periods of remission. I don't mean to be discouraging, but I wouldn't invest much hope in them."

Paul had gone to the waiting room to report to Maria and saw how exhausted she was. She resisted, but Paul ordered her to go home and took her downstairs to put her in a cab. It was three a.m. and there was almost no traffic. They moved off the curb and peered down the avenue for the sight of a cab.

"You'll call me?" she asked for the sixth time.

"Of course I will. But you're done in and I don't want you in the hospital, too."

"If you're sure you don't need me."

"I need you, Maria, but I need you well. Mother's stabilized and there's nothing we can do. If I could have reached Uncle Karly, I would have told him he needn't come. I'll wait until he gets here, tell him what's going on, and come home. Nothing we can do here."

"You're sure?"

"Sure. Ah, here comes a cab."

He went back to the empty waiting room on the sixth floor and sat. He'd gotten used to the numbing anonymity of hospital waiting rooms in the small hours. At first he'd thought of them as much like airport waiting areas, but now they seemed more like train stations that were no longer in service.

He heard the elevator doors *whoosh* and rose. His uncle hurried in breathless and anxious. Paul wanted to embrace his uncle and draw a little warmth, but he knew how much Karly disliked being touched.

Thoughtless with distress, Karly said something to Paul in German, then remembered and asked in his still strongly accented English, "How she is?"

"Stabilized. I tried to reach you when I found out, but you'd already left."

Karly whispered a prayer in German and went to a corner chair into which he dropped his large frame. As always, Karly wore the full costume of a Lutheran minister. No matter what the occasion or hour, Paul had never seen the man wear anything else.

"More suffering she endures. Even for me, it is hard to see the hand of God in this."

"She was like her old self today. No pain, a good appetite. She started to tell me about her life in Germany."

Karly became alert. "She is saying?"

"Did she really get in trouble with the police?"

"Yes."

"And?"

"How much did she tell you?"

"Just about Herne and going to school in Berlin, a couple of men she knew there."

"Rudy and Dieter?"

"Yes. You knew them?"

"I knew Dieter. Did she tell you what she was accused of?"

"We didn't get that far."

"Well, if she must, she must. But there's nothing to be done about any of it. I tried. She got me on the *Queen Mary* back to Germany only three months after the war. Ships came back full with soldiers and sailed away almost empty. I went.

"Getting to Germany, to Berlin, the most awful. All ruins when I got there. Getting to Herne like getting to the moon. No good to do there. A proper marker for Mama and Papa's grave, but so?

"The Red Cross tried for me, but what your mama wanted was not to be done. Too soon, too late?"

Paul's uncle spoke of the chaos he had found, of his own father's resistance to the Nazis in Herne, of losing his church when he refused to join a Nazi state church. But Karly kept returning to Leda's friends, emphasizing how hard he had worked to find them, apparently a little guilty that he hadn't.

Finally, "I think your mama is making a confession about her past. Like that Catholic business."

"Don't Catholics do that to get forgiveness?"

"Maybe your mama wants that. For me, I would make a confession too, if I knew my truth. I don't. And your mama does not know the whole of it. I may have caused your mother's troubles, because I spoke out of turn. I had a young man's conscience then and all it knew was guilt. I was too good the Lutheran, so loving of the punishment.

"Let her tell you, then you come and let me explain me, my part."

"Why all the secretiveness?"

"It is what the Nazis taught us, and they were good teachers. Who does not obey with a gun to the head?"

}

"You know what I don't want, Paul? I don't want my last sight of the world to be this room. All this equipment, 'the ghost of pleasures past' over there. I'd like to be in the garden, stinking drunk on Tanqueray martinis.

"Maria always says I mustn't talk this way. I know it troubles you, but you let me say what's on my mind. It helps."

"Do you want me to fix your pillows?"

She struggled to sit up and said, "Please."

As he fussed the pillows into place she considered him and was struck, as always, by how much he looked like his father. The fact pleased her.

"When you saw Karly, did you ask him about what I'd told you?"

"He made a mystery of a mystery. He said he'd tell me more after you'd told me what you wanted to. He said you were confessing, like a Catholic."

"Nothing that spiritual, I'm afraid. Just the truth. I would imagine one would have to feel one had sinned in order to want forgiveness. If I sinned against anyone, it wasn't God, it was you, my dear."

Chapter 3

Slipping past Nazi prohibitions, modern music still came to Berlin, like money to Switzerland — welcomed, appreciated, and valued — and Leda felt exalted in this universe of music.

Old gramophones in student rooms still crackled through the grooves of Duke Ellington, Bessie Smith, and Billie Holiday, the "race" music now officially discouraged. The young still played the recently exiled Kurt Weill, and, ignoring Party-approved composers, a rebellious teacher took Leda through the rigors of Hindemith's banned music. Her fingers ached from playing it, but she wanted more of its challenge.

Dieter tutored her in popular song and that proved harder than Hindemith. She took easily to Jerome Kern with his classical base, but Gershwin eluded her. She told him it was like teaching a ballet dancer to tap-dance; the disciplines fought one another. Dieter finally figured out she was trying with her mind and hands, so he started each lesson by making her dance while he played. "Just move to it," he told her, and when her body found the music, her playing of it began to take on life.

She was so absorbed in her new life that the birthday card from her parents came as a surprise. The card contained money she knew was more than they could manage and she felt ashamed that she was so greedy for their sacrifice. How long had it been since she had written them? She must. A long letter that would be full of how much she missed them. Tomorrow.

She splurged on a new dress to wear to her September party which Moira had organized with Mrs. Schilling. It was held in the adjoining dining and living rooms of the boardinghouse, and when Leda walked in she was struck by how many people she already knew well and how much pleasure it gave her to see them all together. Rudy had borrowed a phonograph and they danced to new records from America and listened to Gertrude Lawrence sing songs in English from *Treasure Girl*. No one understood a word, but the sound added a satisfyingly worldly air to the party.

At nine the lights were switched off and the blazing cake was carried in to the accompaniment of applause, cries of "Happy eighteenth birthday," and Leda's tears.

The gifts were icing on icing for her, and Leda opened each with delight, exclaiming with pleasure. When the last package was open, Moira said, "Now Rudy has something very special for you, if we can get him away from the cake."

Rudy went into the hall and brought back his cello. He handed Leda a sheaf of music and, as he sat and played his sonatina, she read, "'Sonatina for Leda,' by Rudy Mueller, September 23, 1934. Based on a Bavarian folk song."

She listened, wept, and laughed, joyous to think he no longer thought of taking her to the zoo with his little sister.

৴

Two weeks later they became lovers in Dieter's room on the Kaiser Platz. The room seemed the ideal setting for taking a lover: it was full of fantastically rich fabrics strewn over every surface, reminding her of a set she had seen in a production of *The Tales of Hoffman*. It was a bright room and she delighted in watching him naked, taking this as she took most things in her new life in Berlin, as natural, as part of her delight in the new person she was.

They lay on the bed near the curtained window and felt the cooling October air of late afternoon glide over them.

She asked, "Would you have cared if I hadn't been a virgin?"

"I don't think so. I don't know." He was not being honest and she knew it. He would have cared.

She said, "Making love isn't at all what I thought it would be. I thought it was something a woman had to do, like the dishes or making the bed. That's what Sophie's mother told her. But this wasn't like something I had to do. It's like going into another world, but with someone you trust. It was like being more of myself, being larger but lighter. And I talk too much."

"You do it better all the time."

"What was that thing you put on your billy?"

"My what?"

"Your billy."

"Oh. It's called a condom. It's to keep you safe, so you won't have a baby."

"But I would love to have your baby. Not just any old baby, but your baby. It looked very funny, like a disguise. I almost laughed, but I had the feeling it might spoil things."

"It certainly would have. You must never laugh at a man's ... billy. And where in the world did you get that name for it?"

"I've never seen one, except on bulls and horses, and I had to call it something."

"Billy will do fine."

Dieter fixed the last pin in the fabric and stood, taking the rest of the pins from his mouth and saying, "Now you can turn around and look in the mirror."

Leda turned and saw herself swathed in cascades of Nile green silk. She was struck quiet with surprise; Dieter had transformed her. Dieter moved behind her and pulled her hair back: "You shouldn't have hair around your face. You should show those cheekbones. Your face is ... is what? ... compelling."

"Oh, Dieter, the dress is magnificent."

"And practical. You won't have to fuss arranging it when you sit to play and there are no sleeves to get in your way. You just enter like a baroness and sit."

"How do you know all these things?"

"It's just good sense. Women don't just stand around in clothes, they do things. You play piano."

"This dress will change my life."

"It will bring crowds of men to your dressing room and Rudy will be very angry with me."

"I will have an escort throughout the tour, a nice elderly officer from the Ministry who is supposed to go everywhere with me, like a stern father. I'll only be gone two weeks."

Eight days she would resent being away from Rudy and then five more to resent being at home for Christmas with her family. Only a prized handful more of days with Rudy remained.

"I don't want this tour, but the director says it's good for the school and me to do as the Nazis wish, and it's a tour for their officers which is why I'm getting an escort."

"Stand still while I unpin you and then I'll make us some coffee."

He began to carefully take the dress apart and she watched as it came off in sections, like plates of armor. She said, "I hate watching you take it apart."

"You leave Monday, so you should come for your last fitting on Saturday and I'll do the finishing touches while you wait. And then you can stay on with Rudy if you want. My beautiful shoe salesman and I are going to a Christmas party."

"You really are a lovely friend. Somehow I will get back here for New Year's Eve and buy us excellent champagne and caviar with the money I filch from my tour. We will begin 1935 in style."

⁊

Dieter stitched furiously, his fingers flashing along the hem of her green gown. She watched, fascinated by his skill.

He shouted, "There!" then raised the thread to his teeth, bit, and held aloft her finished dress.

It awed her, for she had seen such splendor only on the most successful performers.

She moved to hug him and he backed away, saying, "Don't muss the dress. Grab that pile of tissue paper and we'll go to your room and I'll show you how to pack this."

He lowered the dress, fold by fold, into a box and they raced out.

As they hurried onto the Unter den Linden, the trees began to scream, the loudspeakers now visible in the bare branches shouting of the imminent passage of Hitler himself. Hordes were rudely shoving their way onto the vast avenue from all directions, then quickly forming orderly crowds that looked with feverish eyes toward the direction from which their Führer, their supreme leader, would come. Police spread their arms and straightened the edges of the mob which obediently aligned itself, reining their disorderly passion into neat ranks for a sight of the man who was giving them back to themselves, giving Germany to true Germans. A man racing by almost knocked Leda to her knees and Dieter saved her from falling. He shouted over the din of the music, "Let's get out of here, before we get knocked flat," and pulled her urgently toward the nearest side street and right into four young SS officers.

"And where the hell do you think you're going?" the largest officer asked, his companions' stern expressions and military bearing underlining his question and his right to ask. "You can lay your girlfriend later, mister. Now you get your ass back there and honor the man whose boots you aren't good enough to lick."

The SS man snatched Dieter's resisting hand and held it aloft. "Jesus, Fritz, just look at this hand. Never did a day's work for his country and he won't even stay to raise his soft paw to honor the master of our age."

As they threatened, they edged toward Dieter, who tried to push the resisting Leda behind him. Dieter knew what to expect, if she didn't, and knew there was no way out. For his lack of patriotic fervor he was to be beaten. Running led to worse. SS beatings of reluctant worshipers of Hitler were now commonplace, never challenged, and approved of by the crowds such brutality attracted.

Leda spun toward the pastry shop behind her, intending to pull Dieter inside, but as she reached for the door handle the shopkeeper, who stood staring out anxiously, locked it and pulled down the shade on which was written "CLOSED." She looked across the way to see other shopkeepers doing the same. Doors slammed, shades fell, lights went out, and the street went blind. They were on their own.

She would never know where the impulse came from, but she pushed between Dieter and the SS man and demanded, "What is your name, Officer? I would like all your names. I would like to give them to our friend Major General Rehlsbach, because you clowns are going to make us late arriving at his home."

They looked confused and the moment's tentativeness blunted the edge of their malice, and Leda seized the advantage.

"Well, if you won't give me your names, I'll remember you well enough and your insignia will help."

Dieter stood dumbfounded.

The soldiers looked confused and began a disorderly retreat, tumbling away at ungainly angles, heading toward the hysterical crowd now screaming at Hitler's approach, but Leda stopped their retreat with a sharply snapped, "Heil, Hitler," which they half returned in stumbling confusion.

Leda saluted back, turned, and tugged Dieter after her, saying, "For heaven's sake, get me someplace where I can sit down. My legs are like rubber. Damned fools! Like children playing some crazy game."

As Leda ran pulling Dieter along behind her, he shouted, "They're not playing."

Once around the corner they slowed a little and Dieter said, "My God, but I was worried about you."

"I was worried about the dress."

⸘

Later, she lay in Rudy's arms and wished the days of her tour and the holiday away, while he did the same. So far, they had not had to endure much time apart.

Home, she thought. Herne wouldn't feel like home, because here and now felt like home. And there'd be no one but Sophie to tell about Rudy, and even that was risky because what if Sophie let something drop and Willy heard, which would mean her parents would hear, and that would lead to...

"What are you frowning about?" Rudy asked.

"Time away from you. But I promise I'll be back for New Year's Eve. How can I see 1935 in without you?"

"We have all the time in the world. I'll be busy at home helping my mother pack to move, and I've promised to help some friends with a project. And I'm behind in my studies. Besides, I've been neglecting all my other girlfriends."

She gave him a smart slap on his bare behind and he grabbed her and held on for dear life, and a little of the tension he'd been hiding from her drained away.

Rudy was glad Leda was going to be away. His news from home was bad: his mother's late Jewish parent had become the subject of active official curiosity, and he had finally talked his mother into moving to France to live with her sister, his little sister having already been sent ahead. And once his mother was safely away he would join some new friends in helping three Jewish students from the Polytechnic cross into Poland on Christmas Eve. Even the Nazis seemed sentimental about Christmas, so might not be as alert at the borders, might even be drunk. He had thought of telling Leda, but why trouble her? Yet, not telling her bothered him. Secrets had never been an issue with any of his other women, but with her they had the nagging edge of a lie, especially since one of his secrets was his shadowy jealousy of her talent and the question of what would happen to them when her career moved so far ahead of his that the gap could no longer be ignored. These conflicts now weighed importantly, because he intended to ask her to marry him on New Year's Eve.

His arms around her tightened and he said, "God, how I'll miss you. Go have a wonderful time. Just come back to me."

≀

"The concerts had gone well and I had enough to splurge on a very expensive bottle of Veuve Cliquot to take back to Berlin.

"I was on the first train out of Essen on December 31. Mother believed my lie about giving a New Year's Eve concert at the school. I remember everything about that train ride in the most incredible detail, because it went on forever. I ached to get back to Rudy.

"Dieter was waiting at the station for me and I couldn't understand how he knew what train I'd be on. He said he'd just planned to spend the day meeting every train from Essen. He wanted to buy me a drink and talk to me he said, but I wasn't going anywhere with a man in tears, so I made him tell me then and there, even with all those people running around the station. New Year's Eve. The place was a madhouse. People rushing to and from trains, some already drunk, noisy, all out of control. And there stands Dieter crying so hard he can't talk.

"He said Rudy was missing. Missing from where or what? I thought Dieter was drunk or playing some awful joke. People didn't just go missing, they had to be someplace. Then Dieter told me about Rudy's helping to smuggle some men out of Germany, across the border into Poland. Students, Dieter said. We had no idea what their names were, so there was no one to call.

"And that's the way my life with Rudy ended. I don't know how many days I ran around Berlin trying to find out what had happened to him. I was warned to stop asking, but you know me. I asked a lot of the wrong people, people who were curious about why I was interested in someone who had disappeared. I was told such questions were dangerous, but I couldn't see how. The director of the school called me in and talked to me about what he called 'the changing times,' explaining, if regretfully, that enemies of the State didn't have to be accounted for and how people who asked for explanations got themselves into great trouble.

"Disappearance is worse than death, Paul. When people die you know the how and why, and time takes care of things. But when a person you love just vanishes they stay alive in your head, not a year older, still wonderful to look at and touch. And that binds me to the young girl I was, because she's still waiting for him. It's terrible to have part of one's self trapped in another time.

"All those books I've been reading have brought it all back. It was Nazi policy to just dispose of unwanted people quietly. No messy, expensive trials. The Nazis called the policy 'Night and Fog.' Sounds almost romantic.

"Come help me up again. I love silk sheets but they're so slippery. I should use good sensible flannel like my mother did."

Paul helped her up and asked, "Is it time for one of your pills?"

"It usually is. With eleven different pills, it's always time. You know what I'd rather have? I'd love a gin martini. If you promise not to tell Maria, I'll tell you where I stash my Tanqueray gin. I'm sure there's still some downstairs.

"I learned to drink gin my first trip to London. I was carrying you when I got there and you just loved gin; quieted you right down."

"Can you drink on the pills?"

"Probably not, but it's hard to care."

He finished making her comfortable and started out to look for her gin.

She stopped him. "Paul?"

"You want something else? Something to eat?"

"Cigarettes. They're hidden in the silver cupboard."

"You have lots of secrets, don't you?"

"Lots."

Leda sipped her martini and thought, Nectar of the gods. She said, "You shocked that your old mother was having an affair?"

"I knew about Mr. Sanders all those years. I thought you'd marry him."

"You never said anything."

"What would I have said?"

"I suppose I'm glad you didn't. There's enough Lutheran left in me to have been ashamed, especially if my son asked."

"Why didn't you marry him?"

"I realized I was past being interested in marriage. His life was here and mine was all over the world. Once I left Herne,

I never stopped moving. I'm one of nature's travelers. It took this damned disease to stop me."

"You miss it." It wasn't a question, but a statement.

"And not finishing the new Bach recordings, not seeing London again, not eating everything in sight, and not and not and not."

She held out her glass. "Please, take this. It's lovely, but it's made me very sleepy. It used to take three of these to put me out."

He took her glass and eased her down. She seemed to be asleep before he finished. He stood over her a long time, until he was sure he could see her breathing.

Hours later she awoke with a start and was immediately aware of the man in the chair. She knew him and said, "Papa?"

He rose and went to turn on a lamp.

"It's Karly. You must have been dreaming."

"No. You look more like Papa all the time. And now you're about the same age as he was when I last saw him."

"Should I go tell Maria to bring up your dinner?"

"Not yet. Just some water. It's over there. We should talk. I've finally got around to telling Paul about my life in Germany. Has he mentioned it?"

Karly nodded. "Are you going to tell him everything?"

"You think I shouldn't?"

"I don't know. Is it important to him or to you?"

"Mostly to me, I think. Paul says you think I'm confessing. Did I ever tell you I once thought of converting to Catholicism?"

"Whatever for?"

"My soul," she said, then amended, "No, only for their confession, for telling someone my secrets, for owning that I still feel I abandoned Dieter."

"To say your own brother had so little charity for a desperate human being?"

"Too late for all that, Karly. I know that Dieter's being the kind of man he was must have been very troubling for you."

"More complicated, Leda. Dieter is still on my conscience too. But I've never known the whole truth about what I did. It is not to be reasoned out, so I must only guess and pray."

"What could you have done? You only saw Dieter twice."

Karly gripped his knees and rocked forward. When he raised his head there were tears in his eyes.

"Oh, Karly, please don't cry. I didn't bring all this up to trouble you. As you say, it was so long ago."

"Paul is here, so the past is with us." When Karly could, he told Leda his secrets, and asked her forgiveness. In another era and country what he had done would have been trivial. In Nazi Germany, in 1935, his actions had been devastating.

It took Leda a long troubled time before she could speak. "Well, Karly, if I'm going to get out of here with any peace of mind, I suppose I must forgive you."

༄

Later that evening, Paul found Leda in the kitchen sipping tea. He made some for himself and sat with her while she finished the story to which she now added Karly's painful portion.

In a way, she wished Karly had kept his secret, because it now seemed even more imperative to her that something be done to make amends to the past.

༄

Rudy was gone and she was driven by Furies to find him. At first she didn't doubt that he was alive, then she was sure he was dead and half-sure she was somehow responsible. If she hadn't gone away for Christmas ... If only she'd asked him about the disquiet she'd sensed in him. The self-damning *If.*

Most awful was the briefly conceived fantasy that he wasn't missing, but had run away from her. She couldn't believe that people just disappeared, even though wiser, informed people were whispering to her that it was now happening all the time and smart people did not ask questions. Dieter knew nothing and became frantic and frustrated that his own perilous position kept him from being of even the slightest help. All she was ever to hear of Rudy was from the secretary of the school's director, who finally risked telling Leda that the SS had requisitioned Rudy's school files early the previous December. Of course they didn't say why; they never did. The woman knew no more and wept bitterly when Leda pressed her. Leda felt too much confusion and rage to weep.

When all her frantic racing about stopped, the best she could do was return, to her music, her classes, and her concerts. She now played regularly on radio, and as the Nazis were intent on seeing that every German family had a radio, her reputation was taking on national dimensions. She was praised and valued by the Party, the school considered her a boon. She had no social life, parties offended her mourning, laughter sounded derisive. All she was able to do with any pleasure was practice and perform.

It was Dieter's danger that brought her back with alarming abruptness to full consciousness.

Dieter called her at school. He didn't say much, but his anguished voice was enough to make her rush from school to meet him at a cafe. She found him at a rear table in a shadowed corner.

"Oh, God, you probably shouldn't even be seen with me, Leda, but I didn't know who else to call. Everyone I know is dangerous to me or I'm dangerous to them. I couldn't think of anyone else I could trust. They're after me, Leda."

She put her steady hand over his trembling one. "Get out of Berlin, go to your parents."

"My parents put me out when they found out I was homosexual. Jesus, Leda, I'm going to go like Rudy, I'll just disappear."

At a loss, she said, "Eat your éclair."

He looked stricken at the idea. "I'm too afraid to eat."

"Dieter, you have to calm down and tell me exactly what's going on."

"Someone told the Nazis where I was living. Probably that awful Kiki I used to work with. I ran into him yesterday. He never had the time of day for me, but he was just so nice. Shouldn't we get together? and how were things going? and where was I living? Like an idiot I gave him my address.

"But, Leda, it was just so nice seeing anyone from back then. Even him.

"This morning I was coming home with coffee and bread, and Mrs. Krindler from next door catches me at the corner of my street and says I can't go home. I couldn't imagine what she was talking about. Well, some men had been by to ask for me and they were still waiting. She said they were not in uniforms, but she was sure they were police.

"I knew my shoe salesman would be at work, so I ran to Rolf's. You never met him. He's beautiful, but he's a shit. We were lovers for a while, so I know and should have known better than to go to him. He could see I was in a state, so I had to tell him what was going on.

"Oh God, he put me out. He's telling me to get out and saying I must hate him to come to him, that I'd get us both arrested. He's yelling at me and pushing me toward the door, and I'm crying like an idiot and asking him to just hold me, let me stay till I calm down. I'm still pleading, but I'm out in the street and the door is closing. Then he's at the window waving me away. It was eerie.

"That's when I called you and that was probably dumb and dangerous."

"Was there anyone else to call?"

"No."

"Then you did the right thing. I'll help."

"How can you?"

"That's what we have to figure out."

"You mustn't, Leda. We're all disappearing. All my old friends. I haven't seen a soul I know, till I ran into that Kiki. People are just gone and we don't even dare ask where. It's as if we're not supposed to notice. Like Rudy. Jesus, I'll be gone like Rudy and only I'll know where I am."

He stopped talking, because he could see Leda wasn't listening. She finally asked, "How much money do you have?"

"Just a little change from the grocery. There's not much more at home. I bought this beautiful bolt of velvet with almost everything I had." To prove his point, he fished the change from his pocket and showed her. Not enough for the food in front of them.

He said, "What's really terrible is that all my beautiful fabrics are back there."

She touched his shoulder in commiseration, knowing they meant more to him than money.

"I have some money," Leda said, "but probably not enough. I don't know who I could borrow from, so we'll have to manage this on our own."

She was thinking out loud when she said, "You'll need a place to stay, clothes. You can't go back for anything." Then to Dieter, "Can you work at the club?"

"I'd be terrified."

"I know, and I'm sorry. Did that Kiki ask where you worked?"

He shook his head and said, "No. I told him I got by doing alteration work for a tailor."

She put her hand on his cheek and he realized it was the first warmth he'd felt all day.

"Is there anyone at the club you could borrow from?"

"A little from Horst, maybe."

"Get as much as you can from whoever you can."

"How would I pay them back?"

"You probably won't."

"That wouldn't be fair."

"Neither is getting arrested for being who you are. Could you sleep at the club for a night or two?"

"Maybe a dressing room. But there's a watchman."

"Give him some money and tell him your girlfriend threw you out. If that doesn't work, you will have to stay in my room," she said and grimaced at the thought of Mrs. Schilling, who prowled at night, listening at doors.

"Do I have to go to work? I'll be too afraid to play."

"Just till I get things organized."

"What things?"

"Who knows? I've never done this before."

"Done what?"

"Hidden a fugitive."

"Can you?"

"No choice, is there? Drink your coffee."

"I can't."

"Yes, you can. You won't go like Rudy. I promise you that will not happen. I am not going to have people I love just taken off to nowhere. Now, for Christ's sake, drink your coffee and eat your éclair."

Here was something she could do for Rudy's memory and when Rudy came back she would have something to tell him that she was proud of, of how she'd honored his memory. She would be able to say, "I didn't cave in like everybody else."

"Now, Dieter, please eat and let me think."

In the next few minutes, Leda found in herself a genius for clear-sighted deviousness that surprised and pleased her. She appraised their resources with cool accuracy, began to think of how to get the most out of them. Within three days, her plan was in effect.

She bought a gold-plated wedding ring, slipped it on, and went to rent a cramped furnished apartment in a run-down neighborhood, under the name of Mr. and Mrs. Dieter Kohl, bargaining the sour landlady down on the rent. She gave up her own room at Mrs. Schilling's, explaining that her aunt had moved to Berlin and her mother insisted she live with her.

She installed Dieter and herself in their new home, provisioned it using what money she had left, and started to look for a way out of the country for him, asking veiled questions of people at school, but without result. For the time, they wouldn't be able to get along without the money from his job at the Blue Wink, so a terrified Dieter reported to work every night. But, in two weeks, his job ended in a frightening encounter when he rebuffed the advances of a drunken army colonel who had bought him a drink between sets. When Dieter didn't show sufficient gratitude, the colonel shouted, "What's the matter, you little faggot? Am I too old for you, not pretty enough?"

"Right on both counts," the distraught Dieter snapped. The colonel stormed out and Dieter got hell from the manager for endangering the club by offending an officer.

When Dieter left that night, three men in army uniforms attacked him and, as he lay bloodied in an alley, one of the men leaned over him and hissed, "That will teach you to keep your filthy faggot hands off an officer."

As Leda cleaned the wounds on his face he cried that he couldn't go back to the club. "It's no good, Leda. That's over. What will we live on? I have no luck. I'm dangerous to be around. I'll just get you into trouble."

"Be quiet. How did you get so much dirt in these cuts?"

"They kicked my face."

"Oh." She touched his hair gently. "We'll work it out. It's only till we can figure out how to get you out of the country."

"There's nowhere to go. I can't work. I can't even use my own name."

"What if we were married?"

"What if?"

"They wouldn't think you were homosexual if you were married. I'd marry you. I do love you. Not like Rudy, but I do."

In answer to her, he wept. When he could speak he said, "You can't make an honest man of me. I've got a criminal record ... the wrong kind."

She put her arm around him and set the bottle of iodine down. She pushed his long hair off his forehead and saw a dirty wound she had missed. She picked up the bottle of alcohol, soaked a wad of cotton, and dabbed gently at the cut, leaning close to be sure she got it clean.

Dieter sat patiently, trying to brave the cleaning silently, tears seeping as he stared at the sorry state of his life. No hope where he was and no exit.

"We'll work it out, because we have no choice," Leda said. "You sew beautifully. I'll find work for you. I'll tell all the girls at school what a brilliant dressmaker I have and bring them to you. And I'll turn professional. I've been saying no to agents who want to manage me. I'll talk to the school. We'll work it out, Dieter."

She spoke with authority and he believed her, as he did almost every night when the fear got into his bones and she comforted him. For her part, she had a purpose in him that was proving as energizing and compelling as her music. She would not lose Dieter, would not allow another human being to be swept away by a force that was ruthlessly expunging everyone who didn't fit the monolithic image of the emerging Master Race.

{

Less than a year earlier, any of Leda's plans for Dieter would have worked well and quickly, but with breathtaking efficiency the Nazis had created a legal system that closed exits to their newly defined undesirables and, while the disenfranchised stood immobilized in the blinding light of the new order, they were scooped up and deposited in bins labeled "politically undesirable," "racially undesirable," or "homosexual." And if some undesirable didn't fit a present category, a new label and bin were hastily shaped by a new law. They didn't want such people in their shiny new hygienically engineered world, but they didn't want them to get out of Germany either. They had plans for them; even undesirables had their uses. They had property and valuables that could be seized as soon as proper laws were passed to make confiscation legal. Additionally, they might benefit the government as forced labor. Some were able to buy their way out with all they owned. Dieter had nothing.

People like Dieter couldn't get a passport, a marriage license, or a job: he had ceased to have any legal status and became a nonperson. All that now remained for the State to do was to gather him up. Leda was harboring an enemy of the Reich and, even if she was becoming what her school file termed "an increasingly valued asset to the State," her danger was as grave as his.

She managed to get Dieter some sewing work to do at home, but the young women she knew at school didn't have much money for fine dresses and the wives of Nazi officials she met at her concerts could hardly be solicited. His old clientele of drag queens were no longer possible customers and, even if they had been, would have been dangerous, since it was known that some, like Kiki, bought their own precarious freedom by informing.

She began her search for an agent, but was told by the school's director that if she became professional, her scholarship would be canceled. She aimed weeping eyes at the school's director and lied: "My parents are too proud to write you, but they've had to stop my little allowance. My father's flock is a poor one and even with so many people working now, they can't go on sending money. Perhaps the school could arrange some private parties for me to play." The director gave her a handkerchief and, within days, arranged engagements and fees exactly as she had suggested. She also set out to find an agent, with no intention of telling the school what she was up to.

With her private engagements, matters got somewhat easier, but never safer. Dieter was afraid to be seen during the day so, weather permitting, they went for walks only in the evening, seeking neighborhoods where neither was likely to be known. Dieter would tease her about her being his mistress and he being the pet she was obliged to exercise, playing – according to his whim – a dachshund, a Weimaraner, or any breed that took his fancy, and talking to her in character, asking her to find him the ideal tree or hydrant or, even better, a lovely fat woman's leg. He improvised imaginatively, making her shriek with laughter. And she would create scenarios for spy movies in which she used her wiles and charms to save him. They found cafes they could afford and shared modest treats that were as good as feasts, sometimes almost forgetting their predicament, but never completely.

One night in late April the weather veered back into bleak winter and they stayed home and cursed their frugality at not buying more kerosene for their small stove to see them though spring. It was proving a painfully chilling economy and they heaped their coats and clothes on the bed and snuggled under, fully clothed. They tried pretending they were Hansel and Gretel watching the witch prepare the oven, but their improvisation lacked spontaneity. Every attempt at talk failed, as they watched their words turn into chilled mist before their faces. They felt abandoned. It seemed a long time for Leda since Rudy had gone and, for Dieter, an eternity since he had been close to his shoe salesman. Dieter's need for love was almost enough for him to forgive the betrayal. So, both in extreme states of cold, loneliness, and self-pity, they made love. As Dieter tumbled off Leda, they both knew it had been an act more full of poignance than of passion.

"See," Leda said later, "we could get married. I thought that homosexuals couldn't make love to women."

"I'm surprised, too. I never have. Probably never will again."

"Did you enjoy it?"

He considered. "It was ... it was nice because it was you." Then he hesitated and asked, "Can I be honest?" and she nodded.

"It wasn't like my shoe salesman, and we're both dressed for a stroll through Siberia."

She nodded in sad understanding. "I kept thinking of Rudy." She blew out her breath and watched it with distaste as it congealed into a crystal cloud. "If I had any courage at all, I would get out of this bed and make us some tea. But I don't. Do you?"

"I'll try, if you'll promise me an éclair tomorrow."

"Worth *two* éclairs. Go!"

He hopped gingerly out of bed and busied himself and she started to giggle because he reminded her of Charlie Chaplin in *The Gold Rush,* all quick jerky movements under his tattered blanket.

She considered their lovemaking and said, "Don't laugh, but have you ever wondered where sex comes from, what makes sex?"

"Never. But maybe from God. Maybe not. Tonight it came from the goddamned weather."

≀

Spring steadied into constant warmth and their nightly walks got later as the days lengthened. It was mid-May when they ran into Dieter's shoe salesman. He couldn't be avoided and, anyway, Dieter couldn't have passed him by. The three stood straining at conversation, then Leda moved off to let them be alone, saying she would wait for Dieter in a nearby cafe. She knew how much Dieter missed the man. But Dieter found talking without touching too painful and brusquely ended the conversation in midsentence, whirled, and hurried away. The man shouted after him, "I'm getting married, Dieter."

His words struck Dieter's back like a rock. He managed to turn and say, "I want things to be wonderful for you," then hurried to find Leda.

≀

In early June, Leda ruefully recalled her cold night in bed with Dieter while sitting across from a doctor. She was there as Sergeant Kraus's wife, having borrowed this persona from a fellow student she couldn't stand, but who was pregnant. This was an important matter, as pregnancies were now closely monitored, to assure that genetically undesirable people didn't have children. So, she sat in the doctor's office remembering that Dieter hadn't used one of those things Rudy had always slipped on.

The doctor praised "Mrs. Kraus" for starting the kind of family the country needed and said she could get dressed.

"You're everything our Führer admires ... healthy German stock," he was saying. "Start early, my dear, make lots of strong children, maybe even win yourself a Mother's Medal with five or six, huh? And what with you having a husband in the SS, your children's futures will be assured. Ask your husband to get you a copy of *Marriage and Racial Hygiene* and you both read it. It will tell you how important your pregnancy is to our country. Good Germans must outbreed the scum that we've been weak enough to let take over."

He talked on and on of racial purity as she dressed. Well, let him. She'd never see the old fool again. But, oh God, she didn't want a baby for herself, much less for the Führer. Would the Führer feed it, look after it? Like hell. This old windbag had bought her story, but she longed to stop his lecture by saying, "I'm a rather easy roundheels, Doctor. In Berlin less than a year and I've forgotten all my parents taught me and been to bed with two men. My baby is the result of subzero temperatures, not racial pride, and the father is a former female impersonator who's in love with a shoe sales-man. And my first lover was part Jewish. You want babies for the Fatherland, you old fart, I'll be happy to bring you mine. What in God's name will *I* do with one? I'm as dumb as that Frieda everybody laughed at back home."

What the hell was he saying now about some Hereditary Health Law Court? Whatever it was, she sensed its ominous importance in his tone. She came from behind the dressing screen and asked him to explain. The doctor burst into a rhapsodic aria about the grandness of the new court's aims.

The court was Germany's latest innovation to keep "unde-sirables" from bearing children. If it were learned that her baby had been fathered by a homosexual, her condition would come under that court's rule. The doctor picked up a pamphlet from a stack he kept at hand and read, "There is complete unanimity in our requirement that sterilization is not to be postponed because the person is pregnant. The ovaries of the woman are to be removed or unbound. Care must be taken to make it as difficult as possible, if not in fact impossible, for surgery to undo this measure. Persons who have been steril-ized must be prevented from traveling abroad in order to have physicians there counter the effect of surgery." And Leda knew that hers was an undeniably anti-Nazi baby.

Leda looked distressed and the doctor patted her fondly, saying, "The law is to protect you and your children, to protect all of us."

"Is this a new law?" He nodded and said, "I helped write that law, my dear, and I did it for fine women like yourself."

She managed a smile, stood, and let him lead her out of his office.

{

Outside, it took only moments for her to know she couldn't tell Dieter about the baby. Why tell him? What could he do? And she didn't give much time to feeling sorry for herself; events had swiftly taken her beyond that.

She hadn't wanted a child, but here it was. Despite her father's calling, she had never been religious, but now she thought about Fate and wondered if that was another of God's names. Well, she would have the child. But how and where? Not here, not Berlin, not even Germany. She had been of no use to Rudy and she knew her protection of Dieter was precarious, and now even more so. The baby was safe as long as no one could see it, as long as it lay curled within her, silent and waiting.

She estimated that probably, at best, she had two months before the baby showed. Well, one way or another, her problems would just have to be managed in two months.

{

She consulted no one until she completed her plans and then wrote her brother, asking him to come to Berlin and sending him money for the trip.

It took Karl two days to arrange the time away. She met his train at 11:45 and took him immediately to the Adlon Hotel for lunch.

"I barely recognized you, Leda. Such smart clothes, such very short hair. And you even look older, more a woman. And this grand dining room. You know, I wouldn't have dared come here by myself. Much too grand, but my little sister looks very at home here. Grown slim and smart, no more baby fat."

Leda laughed very hard at that and thought, Wait! She ordered sherry for them. He said he shouldn't have a drink and she said he should: he'd need it. Karl blanched at the menu prices. He said the cost of one dish would feed a family in Herne for a week, even a month. She shushed his objections. "Eat it and enjoy it, Karly. I'm doing it to soften you up."

Their lunch arrived and was served with an elaborateness that baffled Karl. Such fuss over food, but he ate with dedication.

"Since you wrote to me through Sophie, I take it it's something you can't tell Mama or Papa, but your letter didn't make a lot of sense."

She ordered dessert for them and as the waiter moved away she said, "I'm eating for two." She hid her amusement at Karly's slack-jawed reception of her news under her napkin, then went on: "I shouldn't be, but there it is. And I need your help, Karly. I'm sorry to spring this on you, but I couldn't think of a way to ease into the subject. I seem to be doing everything fast these days. It probably won't even take the baby nine months. You'll have to know it all, if you're going to be of any help."

All he could find to say was, "You are most different. You don't even sound like yourself. You sound hard."

She shrugged and motioned to the waiter for the bill. He brought it on a silver tray, bowing as he presented it. She said, "This is to be charged to Mr. Howe's account. Room 1127. The maitre d' knows."

Karl wanted to know who Mr. Howe was, his first suspicion being that the man had fathered Leda's child.

"He's my new agent from America, Karl. And I want you to be my new manager for a while. I'm going on tour. I'm going to England and then on to America. Managing is not a complicated job. What I most need is someone to see me through what needs doing. You say I'm hard, but I don't think I'm tough enough to do what I have to do by myself."

"You're too young to take all this on."

"Not anymore. Now I want you to meet Mr. Howe. I've told him everything, so we can be frank with him."

"But what about school, Mama, Papa?"

"I've left school. If I go abroad, Mama and Papa will be spared knowing what kind of woman their daughter has become, unless you feel you must tell them."

"But why such a rush?"

"Baby's in a hurry."

"There must be a father."

"He doesn't know and I won't tell him. He's in enough trouble. He can't even help himself, and every day I become less help and more of a danger to him. I'll have to manage this on my own. If these were different times I'd handle matters differently, but if I don't do something fast the law says that the baby will be destroyed and I'll probably be sterilized. I'm not hard, Karly; the facts are. I'm learning to deal in hard facts. Our fine nation can't have a *Lustknaben*'s baby running around corrupting the other tots."

"I don't understand the word you used for this man."

She had to think back over what she'd said. She remembered. "Ah, *Lustknaben*. It's slang for homosexual."

"Which is?"

She searched for a word he'd understand and said, "Sodomite, Karly."

"That cannot be."

"My condition says otherwise."

Karly pressed his napkin to his mouth.

"I was hoping to spare you the more gruesome details, Karly, but I guess they're necessary, if you're going to have any idea of what I'm dealing with."

Leda told Karly the story of her life with Dieter, of Rudy's disappearance, and it took her less time than she would have imagined. Dieter and she had been together only six months but, in the intensity of danger, it seemed like years.

"Oh, Leda, it's so much for me to think about."

"I know, Karly. But I'm out of choices. I'd feel safer with you, but if you can't help, I'll understand. I know you're supposed to start your studies for the ministry in September, so I know how much I'm asking. The baby should be born in January. That would mean a four-month delay for you. I know I'm asking a great deal, but I'll need an answer while you're here."

"I would like to pray about it."

"Of course you will," she said, rising and laying her napkin aside. "Now come meet Mr. Howe."

}

Karl was impressed by Farragut Howe's systematic mind and by his perfect command of German.

"The important thing, Mr. Kohl, is to get Leda out as quickly as possible. First London and the tour of the provinces, then however long it takes in America. I've arranged with your government to sponsor Leda's tour in England. I've assured them that they can make great propaganda capital out of a lovely young talented German woman. Your sister will represent her government and be a fine example of the brilliance of your nation's musical heritage. She'll be sent off with flags flying. There's a nice irony in that.

"I've told Leda that she can have her baby in secret in America and return, but she says not. She wants to keep her child, and that means remaining in America. But once she announces she's staying there, I'm not going to be one of your government's favorite people. It would be unfair of me not to point out that you could have some problem when you come home, but you can denounce Leda as ... what? ... an ingrate, a fool, a bad German."

Karl asked, "And what will happen to my sister?"

"I'll see she's very well cared for. Your sister's not the first German I've helped out of your country."

Karl looked from Leda to Mr. Howe, trying to see if there was more than art and assistance beneath this man's intentions. Despite what had happened, his sister's virtue was still important to him. Karl thought Howe a good-looking man for his years, but he must be at least fifty, more than twice Leda's age. He could also see that Howe dressed well, but Karl's knowledge of the world beyond Herne was scant, so he didn't recognize the Saville Row suit, Charvet tie, or John Lobb shoes that spoke of success and wealth.

"Your sister can have a remarkable career in America, Mr. Kohl. She's beautiful enough to be in movies and that will be a great asset in her concert career. I represent some fine artists and my representation confers some distinction. Your sister's pregnancy is only a temporary event in her life, *if* we get her out of Germany. I don't know your feelings about what's happening in Germany, Mr. Kohl, but I think your country's in grave trouble that will get worse. But that's an American's opinion.

"What I'm trying to do, Mr. Kohl, is assure you that even if you can't accompany your sister, she will be in good hands. But if you can, you can be a great help to her.

"I won't be able to stay in England more than a week and she'd be on her own until she got to America. We don't yet know at what point her pregnancy will preclude her doing any performing. You are needed."

Karl believed Mr. Howe, but as to his own part, he felt badly off balance.

"When will I have to give you an answer?" Karl asked.

"I leave for London in a week. I'd like to know by then, mostly for my own peace of mind about your sister's safety, because I understand the danger she's in. Whether you decide to go or not, you should apply for a passport immediately. I can speed that process up for you. I think we should all treat this as an emergency."

When Karl and Leda were outside the hotel Leda pointed Karl down the Unter den Linden to the cathedral which could be seen rising majestically a few blocks away. "I know you need time to think," Leda said, then added, "And pray, of course.

"Sorry to heap all this on you, but you see the way things are. I'll take your bag with me and you come along to our place when you want. We'll check you into your hotel later. Take your time. Enjoy the day."

How could he enjoy anything? he wondered as he walked toward the cathedral. The clear line that had lain before him all his life had been twisted suddenly toward unknown countries and threatening events. He was being asked to postpone his future, leave his home, travel to alien places.

The great open space of the cathedral was meant to glorify God, but it felt too large for him to find comfort in as he did in his father's small embracing church, so he sat staring into its vast shadowed reaches. Then he fell heavily to his knees and closed his eyes to try and look within himself. He had promised his life to God, not to any person, and not to breaking laws. Now he was being asked to join his sister in breaking the laws of both God and State.

"God, help me," he prayed and repeated this over and over. When he finally opened his eyes there was barely any light coming through the windows.

When Karl rang Leda's bell she came down with his bag and took him to his hotel. She helped him settle in and said that Dieter would meet them at a restaurant near the hotel.

"I should tell you, Leda, that I will be very uncomfortable being seen in public with this kind of man. I do not approve of him or what he does. And as long as I'm saying it, you should know that I am shocked that he should be the father of my own sister's child. It is not right and I can't pretend I find it so."

She had never heard him sound so much like their father and felt as chastened by his criticism as if he were, and as irritated.

She said what she felt she could, without starting an argument: "He's been a wonderful friend and he's a fine man, Karly. As fine as I've ever known. Life would be a lot easier for him if he weren't homosexual, but he is. We've rarely discussed it, because it hasn't been important to me, but I don't think it's something one decides to be, it's just what he is. Treat him the way you'd treat anyone who's been kind to me."

"What is kind about living off you and getting you with a baby?"

"He's always there for me and he never tells me who I am or what I should be, or what I should feel or think. I've never had a friend like that."

"I'll do my best," Karl said, not understanding what Leda had said nor, for that matter, what his "best" might be.

As Karl and Leda walked to the restaurant, Karl returned to the question of how much Dieter knew about her situation and her plans to leave. She was sure she had told her brother everything and wondered why Karl was being obtuse. She curbed a sharp reply and said, "He can't know about the baby, Karly, because he can't help. If he knew, he would try to take responsibility and that could only make matters worse. You may not think it, but things could be worse. All he knows is that I'm going to England and America to perform. I've urged Dieter to get out of Berlin while I'm away and stay near the Swiss or French border where it would be quicker to get him out. Mr. Howe is going to try to pull some strings and, while I'm gone, he'll see Dieter gets money through friends here. I hate myself for not being honest with him, but I can't. I'll have to put it all in a letter and that makes me feel dishonest and disloyal."

"It goes against everything I believe, but this Dieter person should do his Christian duty and marry you."

She was exasperated by his pedantic virtue and answered angrily, "He can't. He's safe because they can't find him. Do listen, Karly. For Christ's sake, listen! This is not about God; this is about Nazis who want to murder him and my baby."

⟩

Karl looked at Dieter's extended hand for a long moment before he could bring himself to take it, as if the act bound him to a contract or commitment or, as Leda thought watching his hesitancy, as if he feared he would be contaminated. She hated what she thought his reticence implied and, if she hadn't needed him, would have told him to get the hell out. Dieter was more used to such heterosexual reserve and could accommodate the implications, even ignore the pain it gave him. Besides, this man was Leda's brother and she had spent time the night before trying to make Dieter understand that her brother was unworldly. If this man was important to Leda, that was what mattered. He would charm this stern young man for her sake.

Conversation was constrained and when the menus arrived Karl held his like a shield. He prayed to God to get him through. When he could, he put his menu down and asked Dieter, "What will you do while my sister is away?"

"Miss her. You see she walks me every night. Otherwise I'm stuck at home. Our landlady thinks I'm recovering from an illness."

"I don't think she believes it. She's a nosy gossip, which is why I want you to get out of Berlin, Dieter."

"Where do I go? These days, you need papers to cross the street. I don't have any identification and they check people constantly. They stop people on the street for no reason and ask to see their identification. Everybody on a train is checked. I don't know anyone with a car I could trust."

"Mr. Howe could see to a car and driver."

"And once I get to wherever?"

"I wish I could send you to my parents," she said.

"That would be out of the question," Karl barked. "A man like him. What are you thinking, Leda?"

"Please, don't be angry with Leda, Karl. I know you don't approve of me and I know it would be so much better for me if I could be different. But even with all the trouble of being who I am, if I tried being something I'm not, I think I'd feel dead."

"For God's sake, Dieter, don't defend yourself. You don't owe anyone an explanation for who you are. And Karl, this is my friend and that's that. I'm not asking you to approve of anything. I think we should order and I think I'd like a schnapps." Karl pursed his mouth but said nothing. He no longer knew his sister; this was a strange woman. He wasn't hungry. He wished he were home, out of this immoral city, free of his sister's frightening needs. He felt dangerously out of his depth. He knew of sin and man's fallibility, but the people he knew were repelled by sin and aspired to God's forgiveness. They didn't pretend sin was anything less than an abomination. His sister and this man accepted terrible transgressions as if they were simply to be accommodated or gotten around. Worse, they expected his tolerance. His presence here, even thinking of helping them, was in itself the stuff of sin. He longed for understandable country sins, not the blazing urban ones he saw being flaunted before him. He should get up and leave, go home, leave this unrepentant pregnant woman and this terrible man, but he stayed. What he couldn't admit was that he was in the grip of a fevered fascination for them, fixed in place by these exemplars of sins only hinted at in his theology. Should he stay and pray to find God's will for himself with them? Was it his Christian duty to try and save them from themselves? Just when he needed his father's counsel most, he couldn't ask for it.

Karl came out of his reverie to find his food barely touched and Dieter and Leda in intense conversation. "I'd just ask them if you could," Leda was saying and Dieter answered, "I'd even play them the goddamned 'Horst Wessel Song' to get my hands on it." Karl saw that their attention was fixed on a battered piano near the bar. "If you don't ask," Leda said, "I will."

Dieter went to the bar. Karl couldn't hear what he said, but he saw the woman behind the bar look delighted. Dieter went to the dilapidated piano, opened it, pulled up a chair from a nearby table, and began to play a Strauss waltz. He finished and sat staring down at his hands with disapproval. He shook them as if to shake off the cobwebs he felt and resumed, playing a medley of songs from *The Merry Widow*. Leda smiled at Karl, inviting him to share her pleasure, but he continued to look into his plate. He didn't see her disdainful shrug as she got up and went to sit beside Dieter. Karl heard her say, "Play some Gershwin," and Dieter answer, "If you'll play some Chopin."

Karl tried to eat, but the food was now cold. He watched as the other patrons gave pleased attention to the attractive pair at the piano and saw the woman at the bar bring them snifters of brandy. My God! How could they make such a display of themselves? Couldn't the people here see what kind of man Dieter was? To make himself so public, and with his sister. But Leda had no shame, was no better. He didn't notice that the music sounded wonderful, even on that much-neglected old piano.

Leda put her hand on Dieter's shoulder as he played and watched his hands scamper in pleasure. He got inside the music and danced around in it, and she could feel the joy. Dieter finished, bowed to the applauding patrons, and introduced Leda who sat and played Chopin's "Heroic Polonaise" energetically. She finished, rose, and they both stood and bowed with self-amused aplomb to the warm applause. They felt exhilarated.

They returned to their table to find Karl gone. Let him go, Leda thought. If I have to go to England alone I will. I've gotten this far. To hell with him.

"I'm sorry he didn't like me," Dieter said.

"I'm not."

}

It was late, and the streets were nearly empty and very dark. Karl had been sure he could find his way back to his hotel, but he was lost. That didn't bother him nearly as much as the wrenching emotion that made him step into a doorway and turn from the street to hide the tears that came in a spate.

The next day Karl came to Leda's school to find her and apologize. "I was tired and it had been a difficult day. I still haven't made up my mind, but I applied for my passport this morning. That's the best I can do for now, Leda. I think I would like to see your friend again. I was unkind to him. I was un-Christian."

Leda said she understood, thanked him for saying he was sorry, and hugged him, relieved to be able to be fond of him again. She knew she might well be asking more of him than he had to give. He was probably doing his best, but she could see the sharp contrast in their reactions to what was happening. I've changed, she thought, then corrected herself: No, I'm just more different than I suspected; I'm starting to be who I really am.

Karl found a small church and spent much of the day there trying to calm his racing thoughts and the new feelings that were taunting him, just out of reach and sight, but both exciting and repellant. For once, prayer proved no refuge, although he prayed with an intensity that matched his careering emotions. He prayed because he was sure his soul was in peril. He prayed to be saved from what was worst in himself, from what would damn his soul for all eternity.

Leda arranged another dinner for them. This time, instead of being disapproving, Karl seemed almost deferential toward Dieter. Sadly, Karl was able to see his own isolation in their easy intimacy. Karl had no talent for easy comradery and remained a self-contained stranger.

At Leda's urging, Karl said he would have one drink and Leda ordered him a schnapps, showing him how to drink it when it arrived. "You snap it back, get it down in one quick gulp." He did as he was told and the liquor shot into his empty stomach and coursed through him. His cheeks reddened, and his ears buzzed. Then, amazingly, Leda and Dieter seemed to move closer to him, more real and warm.

Leda was surprised that the change in Karl showed so visibly and ordered him another drink, and then another, saying, with his third, "Now that you're used to it, Karl, you should sip this one."

They ate heartily and Karl felt at one with them. For the first time in his life he no longer lingered at the edge of intimacy. His barriers of reticence were breached by the powerful schnapps. He ate well and with pleasure, and laughed at their jokes, even when he didn't get them or thought they might be naughty.

As they walked from the restaurant, Karl had the odd feeling that his feet had grown farther from his head and required concentration to make them behave properly. He walked next to Dieter and when their shoulders touched he felt a flash of heat run down his arm.

At the corner where they parted, Karl kissed Leda on the cheek. Dieter stood aside. Then Karl suddenly spread his arms in what looked like a gesture of flight and lurched to embrace Dieter, but Dieter looked frightened and stepped back. In that retreat, Karl saw Dieter's fear of him and felt shamed by his own demeaning need to hold this man close, to feel the weight and solid warmth of him.

Karl wheeled and ran. Dieter and Leda shared a brief, quickly averted glance, neither wanting to acknowledge what had been so glancingly implied. They didn't move on until they could no longer hear Karl as he ran.

Karl sped along without direction, escaping the terrible visions of what his body wanted and his mind was repelled by.

He was feverish with shame, and prayed and wept as he ran.

≀

Karl kept his promise to Leda and picked up his passport, which, with Mr. Howe's help, had been hurried through. He felt a childlike delight in having this official adult document and was struck by how young he looked in his picture, because he always felt himself so much older, old enough to be his father's brother. The young man in the picture had the same large candid eyes as his sister, and his face had the same foxlike shape, broad at the brow and running in arced lines to a point of chin. The main difference was that he was as fair as she was dark.

He was to meet Leda for lunch, but he had made a very early appointment and hurried to the cathedral where he sat in the front pew reviewing his decision one last time. He needed the strength to run from this occasion of sin, his sister and her seductive friend. He needed the advice and support of a more experienced clergyman, but would tell the man only what was necessary.

He rose from his knees and went to the cathedral's manse to meet the clergyman he had called that morning.

As Karl spoke to the man, he felt assured that the pastor shared Karl's shock at Leda's condition and companion. An immoral, even illegal, state of affairs, the man agreed. The pastor said it was the State's work to regulate the irregular and, happily, the State's aims and contemporary Christian thought were as one in this affair. Something should be done about such people. Questions were asked and answered. He counseled Karl to love the sinner and despise the sin, but not to aid Leda by going with her. He gave Karl his blessing and they knelt together in lengthy prayer.

Over lunch with Leda, Karl came right to the point: "I have prayed and sought spiritual counsel, Leda, and I can't go with you. It's not the right thing for me to do. But it makes me sad. You've never asked anything of me and when you do I can't help. I prayed very hard to be able to, but I can't feel it's God's will for me."

"It was a lot to ask, Karly, but don't worry; Mr. Howe will see I'm taken care of. It means a lot to me to know you tried."

"Won't you go see Mama and Papa before you leave?"

"I'd end up telling them everything. Have you ever been able to keep a secret from them?"

"That's because you shouldn't. They have earned our confidence. What you have done and will do is dreadful. Papa would..."

"Oh, for Christ's sake, Karly, I'm trying to decide who's going to die, the baby or Dieter. If I stay abroad to have the baby, Dieter probably disappears or dies. If I stay and they catch Dieter and me, I'll be aborted and sterilized. Then we'll both be criminals and probably end up in one of the camps. I may change my plans, too. I can go to England and have an abortion. Then I might be able to come back and help Dieter. It's chancy, but maybe worth a try. But that's if Mr. Howe can't find a way out for Dieter."

"You would pay with your soul for this Dieter?"

"What may finally decide me is that I don't know this baby, but I do know Dieter and love him.

"So, what do you hear from God on all this, Karly? Has He been whispering in your ear? Don't you think you should tell me?"

Karl fell back on what he had read: "People are not dying in the camps. They're taken there for a while, till they can be made to see why their actions are so bad for the State."

"No, Karly, they're dying in them. We're hearing it from people who should know."

"That can't be. The Nazis have assured the clergy. They send Papa information to counteract the vicious rumors."

"Well then, I've nothing to worry about," she said in a tone ripe with sarcasm. "We're all going to be just fine."

She turned away. "Go back to Herne, Karly. You're useless to me."

"What will you do?"

"What I have to. I can't afford the luxury of your conscience."

She threw some money on the table, stood, and walked angrily away. He followed.

They walked silently through beautiful streets lined with handsome shops, seeing nothing, he knowing there was no more he could say that she would listen to, she glacially remote. When Leda turned toward her home, Karl followed. He felt he should say he was sorry, but that would be a lie, so he prayed for both of them, that they both be given God's peace. Leda prayed he'd go away before she said something irrevocably damaging.

They turned into a street lined with markets and Leda fished a list from her crowded handbag and headed toward a stall heaped with lustrously fresh vegetables. As they neared the stall Leda saw her landlady, Mrs. Boetger, and waved.

What happened next occurred with such devastating speed that Leda could only stand and stare as Mrs. Boetger screamed at her, "How dare you! You terrible woman, you slut! You're out of my home and you'll stay out. How could you, you unholy creature? And is this man another one of them? To have my neighbors see such a thing at my house. Police at my door. My husband died for his country in the Great War and you bring dishonor on his widow. My God, they even wanted to take me to the station to give evidence. Me, a good woman in a place like that, and all because of you. They told me all about him and I told them all about the two of you. Don't think I don't know you've missed two periods. You're going to have a baby. You think I don't know what goes on in my own home?"

Mrs. Boetger became aware of the gathering audience and it gave energy to her righteous outrage.

"And if you think you're getting your things out of my home you're mistaken. Not until I know what awfulness you've done there. You owe me a lot for this. A hero's widow has rights and will not be abused by the likes of you. And he'll get what he deserves. The police will see to that. They're finally getting rid of the scum and your friend will be kept with his own kind, away from good people. They should lock all the homosexuals up once and for all. I'll never be able to go into that room again knowing what must have gone on in there. That awful man of yours is in jail where he belongs and where you belong, you tramp."

Leda had been backing away from the enraged woman, but she was stopped by the large curious crowd that now walled her in. The crowd waited expectantly for Leda to answer the screaming woman's charges and continue the fascinating drama, but all Leda could do was gape and try to hold down her rising panic.

Karl seized Leda's hand, crashed a passage through the crowd, and tugged her behind him, while Mrs. Boetger tried to follow, eager to spend the rage that had gathered in her since the police had come to arrest Dieter, and had dragged and beaten him into the waiting police wagon.

Karl drew his dazed sister along, going faster and faster, hearing Mrs. Boetger screaming, "The police want you! The police will get you, you slut!"

{

"The only good thing about what happened is that it didn't leave me time to think. If I had, I probably wouldn't have made it out. I might have gotten it into my head I could help Dieter.

"Karly said he would tell you more about that pastor he spoke to in Berlin, but how much more can there be that's worth knowing? But the man who was betrayed was your father and you may feel differently.

"Karly says he's prayed ever since and he still hasn't found peace. What may be worst in all this is that Karly may have wanted to hurt Dieter, because of what he started to feel for him. Hardly a new story, Paul, just ugly as ever.

"The more I think of it, the more I wish he hadn't told me. But I guess he had to tell someone.

"It's forty years and the awfulness is still alive. Christ, who needs hell when you have people like the Nazis."

Then Leda fell quiet for so long that Paul looked closely to see if she'd fallen asleep. Her head was bent and she was staring at her hands, which lay in her lap. She had gone back in time. Then she awoke to the present and asked, "Where was I?"

He had to think before he said, "Running from that woman."

"Ah, yes. Well, like most crises in my life, I became focused on some irrelevant detail, and what I remember most of that scene in the street is the head of lettuce Mrs. Boetger was waving around while she screamed. I can't remember her face, but I can still see that perfectly gorgeous head of lettuce.

"Karly got me back to the Adlon. Mr. Howe called a lawyer friend, but the man was a Jew and he told Mr. Howe he'd find him a Nazi lawyer. He found out that Dieter was being held without bail, but had no idea where.

"What worried Mr. Howe was what Dieter might tell them about me. I didn't think he'd say anything, but Mr. Howe said we couldn't be sure and I'd better get out of Germany right away. He had me on my way to Paris that afternoon and Karly came with me after all. Karly was just going to stay with me in Paris till Mr. Howe could come along, but once we were moving, he just kept on with me. Oddly, not a peep out of the Nazis about my leaving. Probably glad to be rid of me without any bad press.

"Then came America, living in this house, and the recording contract with RCA, all of which was wonderful. I needed money. You were almost due and Karly had no English, so he couldn't get work. I recorded a flashy album of three 78s, all showy pieces like Iturbi played, and did radio concerts. Mr. Howe invented a husband for me back in Germany to explain my increasingly obvious condition.

"Since pregnant women didn't play public concerts in those days, eventually I could only do radio. You arrived right after a concert on NBC I barely made it through. But there was a hundred-dollar fee and even you weren't going to keep me from getting it. I just sat there and banged out the Rachmaninoff, and I never played it better. Contractions do wonders for Rachmaninoff.

"I brought you here from the hospital and, the day we returned, Mr. Howe proposed. I'd guessed he would and I had decided to say yes. He'd been married three times to other musicians, so I couldn't figure out why it was taking him so long to propose. He certainly had enough experience. He'd never had a child and he was completely in love with you. He could hardly stand to be away from you. I half think you were why he married me.

"I didn't love him as I'd loved Rudy, but I was very happy with him and I think I was good for him. I know he was good for me.

"I went back to studying and concertizing, and I was something of a hit right off the bat. All this had happened by the time I turned twenty.

"As to Dieter, he just stayed lost. Mr. Howe kept after the lawyer in Berlin, but the man got nowhere, or said he didn't.

"Then we were in the war and Mr. Howe was able to activate his World War I commission. So, by my late twenties, I was a widow.

"After Karly got back from looking for Rudy and Dieter in Germany after the war, I gave up. Like everyone, I just wanted to put the war behind me.

"Now I've gotten it into my head that Dieter may be alive. It's probably the pills, or guilt, or too much time to think about the past, but there he is. I look at you and there he is. You're remarkably like him.

"I'll probably never know the truth about him, but you could. What I want, Paul, is your promise to try and find Dieter. I'm not asking because he's your father; that might be wrongheaded of me. How could I begin to imagine what you might feel for someone you've never known, might not even want to know?

"I guess what I'm asking is that you try and make up for what I wasn't able to do.

"If he can be found, I'd like you to be sure he's taken care of, see he gets the half million if he needs it. If he's dead or you can't find out the truth, give the money to charity. But settle the matter for my sake."

Paul had ridden the emotional tides of his mother's story and, by now, had lost his sense of direction. Should he resent her lying all these years, or hate his uncle for duplicity, or care about the fate of some stranger who was his father?

"I don't know what to say. I feel overwhelmed. I can't figure out how I feel about any of this."

"How could you?"

"Why did you wait until now to tell me all this?"

"When you were born, no good woman had a child out of wedlock. Illegitimacy was a shame that could ruin a child's life. When I was growing up, young women who had a child without a husband were sometimes driven from Herne. If their families stood by the girl, they took on her disgrace and were shunned. Those are powerful lessons when you're young."

"I wouldn't know where to start to find Dieter. It's forty years. I suppose he'd be your age."

"Four or five years older."

"Early sixties, then."

"It's hard to imagine him old. It's hard enough for me to believe the face I see in my own mirror."

"Even if I did find him, what could I tell him?"

"That I always remembered him with love and missed him. That I ran to save my life and yours, and I've always felt something of a coward about doing that. Since he didn't know I was pregnant, you don't even have to tell him you're his son. Or tell him, if you want. That's not for me to say.

"I'm sorry to leave you my mess. It's a helluva legacy, isn't it?"

"Mr. Howe was always my father and my hero. Now I have a homosexual father, because you ran out of kerosene. It's absurd."

"That's one of the things I've always liked about life. But let's say he is alive. Do you think you'd want to meet him?"

"God only knows. Just thinking of him as my father feels weird. Let's put it another way, Leda. Would you want him to know I was his son?"

"Good question." She thought before she said, "I have no idea. It would depend, wouldn't it?"

"You've given me one helluva puzzle, Mother."

"I didn't mean to. It's just that I keep picturing Dieter alive and poor. He wasn't very good at looking after himself. As to his knowing he's your father, that will be up to you. He may not want a son and you might think he was one father too many. All that's important to me is that he know I never stopped caring about what happened to him."

Paul's Journey

New York, Berlin, Munich
1975

Chapter 4

At thirty-eight years old, Paul learned that there's no use preparing for death's assault and that, where most of life's events allow for alternatives, death deals in absolutes. He discovered that choosing a coffin isn't done by decision, but by baffled grief, and that asking about cost makes one feel shabby, so that price is determined by confusion and cowardice. He found that the relief he imagined he was finding in sleep was illusory, because he awoke exhausted. He found how helpless one was to ease the pain of others, for nothing he did eased Maria's grief. She wandered from day to day, looking as if she'd just crawled from a terrible accident.

His soon-to-be-ex arrived at the house to offer solace and unasked-for advice, and was sent away with furious dispatch. His own words surprised him: "You can come pick over the bones in a few weeks. But right now I want you the hell out of here and I don't want to see or hear from you, until I tell you."

As he was pressing her out the front door, she was protesting that she meant well, had loved Mother Howe, and was only trying to help.

He asked himself what he had ever seen in that woman, and answered, Bones, breeding, and an end to intermittent celibacy, and then returned to his chores without another thought for her.

The list of what he needed to do was enormous. There was Maria to be settled in Philadelphia. He'd promised to help her buy an apartment near her sister and get her moved in. There was the house to be cataloged, appraised, and emptied, an apartment for himself to be found, the office to be reorganized and, perhaps, closed, his mother's papers to be sorted, and on and on. And it all felt equally imperative, as if it must all be done at once, like the Big Bang. Among those imperatives was the question of Dieter Holtman.

Leda's funeral service was performed in Karl's church, St. Peter's Lutheran in Brooklyn Heights. Karl conducted a brief service that was small and private, with only a handful of Leda's intimates invited. Paul knew Leda hadn't wanted any service, but didn't tell his uncle, for fear of hurting his feelings or giving the impression that Leda was angry with him over what he had told her about his part in Dieter's disappearance.

When Leda's friends in the music world found out the family planned no memorial service, they took it on themselves to organize one at the Friends' Meeting House on East Fifteenth Street and to advertise the event. Paul was invited and lived in dread of the day. It proved to be as awful as he'd expected. He steeled himself to get through it and arrived home with almost no memory of having been there.

Paul had no idea Leda's death would create so much commotion. The *New York Times* carried a half-page obituary, there was extensive TV coverage, numberless radio tributes, and endless phone calls. Using her several languages, his secretary handled most of the inquiries from abroad. However, a reporter from the German magazine *Der Stern* insisted on speaking to Paul. The woman spoke excellent English in an overly precise voice that seemed to put everything she said in italics.

"I've been working on a story about Madame Kohl and I've come across the same rumor twice. It is that Madame Kohl was forced to leave Germany because of some difficulty with the police. Is that why she never returned to play? I would like your confirmation and, that failing, some comment."

Paul took a breath and answered evenly, "That idea's news to me. If you find anything out, I'd be interested to hear it and I'd be happy to comment."

"Then it is not true?"

"That's not what I said."

"You do not think it worth pursuing?"

"If it will help your story, by all means follow it up. I have no objections. I just don't know anything."

"Then I will look elsewhere for help."

"I wish you luck. I would appreciate getting a copy of the issue that carries your story on her."

"It will be my pleasure."

Paul hung up and thought, Good. Perhaps she'll find something that will help, because I have no idea where to start.

⟩

It was seven weeks before he awoke one morning and realized he felt rested. It was the first day he felt he might actually be able to do all that needed doing.

He spent the morning touring the house with a woman from Sotheby's auction house, discussing the pieces Sotheby's would take and which would be sold in major sales and which in the Arcade sales. In the afternoon he talked with his secretary about her taking charge of the office for a month or so. Finding he'd finished earlier than expected, he called and invited his uncle to dinner.

For the first time in over six months, he felt able to listen to one of his mother's recordings. The record player was in the sitting room where his mother had spent her last days. He hadn't gone into the room since his mother had been carried from it and he had sat at the bottom of the staircase watching, but not believing.

With a fortitude he couldn't begin to understand, the day after Leda's death Maria had cleaned the room, had the hospital rental equipment company remove the rentals, and restored the room to its original appearance. He knew it would look uninhabited, but there would be the ghosts of parties and laughter, Christmas trees, music. He was sure Leda would linger there, because she had loved the room.

He reached for the doorknob and felt as if he were reaching into fire. He went in and was surprised to find no ghosts. It had returned to being just another room and the only aura was the evocative scent of Maria's lemon-scented polish. The room had regained its serenity. He riffled through dozens of Leda's recordings before deciding on Schumann's "Kreisleriana," pieces his mother and he loved, but that had sold poorly and were out of press. She had thought their playing to be among her best work and Paul thought it would be a nice tribute to have the recording pressed privately and sent to her friends. He made a note to himself in the notebook he now always carried, then put the record on the turntable. The music brought back his mother like a comforting hand. How many children had the gift of a mother's music?

The books Leda had bought on the Nazi era were in six piles on the library table. One by one he checked the indexes looking for references to homosexuals and found none, except for the Doyle book. Well, some education in the era might help, so he began to read about a country and age that still had the power to bedevil lives.

{

He took his uncle to Hoffer's in Yorkville, because it was the last of the restaurants in the German neighborhood that had high-backed booths that provided privacy. Paul brought a pad to make notes but, as it turned out, there wasn't anything to record.

His uncle couldn't remember the address of the flat Leda and Dieter had shared. The hotel he'd stayed in was gone, as was Leda's school with, undoubtedly, all student records.

"I might have your mother's last address in Berlin somewhere. Your mother was always teasing me about my never throwing anything away, but, you see, one never knows when it is needing.

"But her building, her old street is probably gone. When your mama sent me back after the war, I couldn't find a landmark. Just rubble and people trying to clear it or find something of value in it.

"That great city was almost gone. Then the Allies chopped Berlin up into their sectors. Her old place may be with the Russians. I give your mama's good heart credit for still caring, but it must be hopeless."

"I'm still going to try."

"Why?"

"Because it was important to Mother."

"Is that a good enough reason?"

"Oh, yes."

"Did your mama tell you everything?"

"Yes."

"You know my part?"

"Yes."

"When I told your mama, it felt I was confessing to murder. It was not easy to admit I'd been the cause of such awfulness. Here was I getting ready to preach God, without looking into my own heart to see His will and truth. So, after your mama and I are running, I keep wondering, Was I like Dieter? You understand what I mean? And if I was, then what? I didn't dare find an answer, so I became alone, a man without wife or any love. I look in my heart now and I still don't know my truth, except to know it's too late for such questions. But maybe that was God's will for my life, this solitude. But if I am honest, I think I did what I did from fear. That is not my excuse, Paul, but it is my cross. Still, there is much in a life for which there is no answering.

"There was a German philosopher named Kneber who wrote of 'a murderous and malicious goodness' that he said let man do evil with a good conscience. When I read that, I saw myself and wept. I copied it out and kept it in my wallet until it fell apart. It told me I should be less godlike and more a man among men. I no longer worry about being good, I try to do good and take people as I find them."

"I don't know what to say, Uncle Karly."

"God is also silent on the matter, but I like to think His silence is consent."

Karl forked up a slice of bratwurst, dipped it in mustard, and smiled. "Like home," he said.

"You find Dieter, you can tell him about what I did. Ask him to forgive me and, if he can find it in his heart, to pray for me. Even if he isn't a Christian or doesn't believe in God, you tell him to give me a prayer."

Christmas and the New Year came and went, as the settling of Leda's large and complicated estate crept along. By March, Maria was living in Philadelphia and the house was empty enough to echo disturbingly, and Paul could see how much in need of paint and repair it was. The real estate agents who trooped through with customers said its condition wasn't important, that anyone who paid its price could easily afford to put it back in shape. His lawyer wrote to say Paul's divorce was final. Paul threw the letter on his desk and shrugged away his last interest in the woman.

He bought a three-bedroom apartment for himself in a new building only two blocks away and decided to move his office there by knocking down a wall between two of the bedrooms to accommodate several file cabinets and two desks. He gave his secretary a substantial raise, the title of "rights manager," and left more and more of the running of its affairs to her.

As other concerns eased, he became absorbed in the question of Dieter. When he'd told his mother he didn't know any homosexuals, she looked at him to see if he was making a joke. He wasn't, so she named three symphony conductors he knew, two composers, several eminent performers, and one of his best friends.

"But they're almost all married," Paul objected.

"I only named the married ones to make a point. You expect the obvious; extravagant gestures, high voices, some mincing travesty of a female. And to think I brought you up to be worldly."

"You disappointed?"

"You just need a little rounding out. You like Christopher Knowles. I'll call him and ask him to give you a crash course."

"In what?"

"Gay people. Gay life."

"Won't he think it odd? I do."

"Not coming from me."

"Frankly, Mother, I'm not sure I'd want to be alone with him."

"You think you're irresistible, that he wouldn't be able to keep his hands off you?"

"You said he was homosexual."

"Because you're heterosexual, does that mean you're ready to leap on every woman you see because you're straight?"

"Straight?"

"Slang for heterosexual. You mean that being in a room with Doris Lefertz or Bibi Cohn would drive you to uncontrollable lust?"

"Christ, no."

"But you're straight and they're women. You mean to tell me your sex drive isn't indiscriminate?"

"You're laughing at me."

"No, dear, just being very amused. You think homosexuals crave sex with every man they see. Christopher has had a lover for fifteen years. I believe they're monogamous. But if you think Christopher wouldn't be able to control himself in your alluring presence, we'll forget it.

"I know a lot of Christopher's friends. I've been to wonderful parties at his house. I would have asked you, but you'd have wanted to bring that prune to protect your virtue."

"Am I that much of a Puritan?"

"I'm afraid so and I can't imagine where you got it. Is there a Lutheran gene? I had such wonderful times at Christopher's. I played my Gershwin and Porter. I was best known for my singing of 'Miss Otis Regrets.' God, how I wish I could sit at the piano and sing it for you. Show you a whole new side of me. Why didn't I do a recording of popular music? I play it damned well."

"You surprise me."

"That's the big problem of being a mother. You get stuck in the part. You're afraid to be too much fun around your children or they won't take you seriously. I'm sorry you missed that part of me. My fault."

"You were a wonderful mother."

"Now I wish I'd been less of one and more myself. Well, at least you're learning some of the dirty truth about me. You think about meeting Christopher. If you're afraid for your virtue, you can meet him at a restaurant."

"What could he tell me?"

"That his difference is only sex."

"That's a big difference."

"You think so? I don't. I don't want you to answer, but how important was it with your wife? Could it have kept you married? Was there love? More importantly, was there intimacy? I was always struck by the remarkable courtesy between you two. It seemed so civilized and cool.

"I don't mean to shock you, Paul, but there was almost no sex with Mr. Howe, but there was intimacy and that would have kept me with him forever. It's what I had with Dieter, what I had with Rudy. It's why I still miss all three and love them. I'd wish anyone sensational sex, but intimacy is a greater gift. But perhaps you never learned it from me, because I kept my secret. Secrets require a certain amount of distance, if they're to be secure. Sadly, they're usually not worth keeping.

"Think of it, Paul. We're finally being intimate. No secrets and no holds barred. That leaves me freer to like you better, even love you more than I thought possible. And all because my odd little secret isn't between us anymore."

"You've been doing a lot of thinking."

"What else can I do? I went charging out of Berlin and haven't stopped to think since. Never time. Thinking's not nearly as bad as I thought it would be. Actually, I find I rather enjoy it. I've even been thinking about Berlin, sorting out what was wonderful from the awfulness. The end of that time may have been dreadful, but every memory I have of Rudy and Dieter is full of pleasure."

Paul didn't like thinking about Dieter, but his promise to his mother remained a powerful commitment, so in early April he called his travel agent and made plans to leave for Berlin the first week in April.

Chapter 5

Paul felt marooned on the island of West Berlin, the half-city surrounded by Russian-controlled East Germany, the result of the bad bargain the Allies had cobbled together after the Second World War. Paul was nagged by an awareness of the wall that traveled like an ugly scar wandering across the once-magnificent metropolis.

He was disappointed by his gloomy reaction to the city. He had half expected that his mother's stories and his own reading about Berlin would conjure up the long-gone city and he would experience it as his mother had. This facsimile of Berlin was as the past forty years of war and occupation and division had made it, a relic of itself lived in by only the very young and very old, other ages having fled elsewhere to seek whole lives. Berliners were citizens of an illusory capital.

He stayed at the luxurious Am Zoo Hotel and hired a guide-interpreter. He and his guide called on the police and were directed into a labyrinthine bureaucracy from which they emerged empty-handed. Records were in Nuremberg where they'd been brought for the War Crimes trials, or scattered among the occupying French, British, Russian, and American military officials.

One man arrested in 1935, you say. Who arrested him? SS? Civilian authorities? Special court?

You say you don't know?
Well then, tell us, what was he charged with?
You don't know that either?

As days passed, Paul knew less and less, except that his quarry receded. More and more, he sensed that Berlin had not only been bombed to rubble, but hopelessly fragmented by its occupiers. It didn't seem possible to accomplish anything here.

He walked in the Tiergarten and wondered at the improbable hill there that soared twenty stories high. In flat Berlin it was a mountain made of war rubble. If the old Berlin was anywhere, it was in that hill that contained the city his mother had known and the streets she had walked.

Uncle Karly had found the address of the house Leda and Dieter had shared, but it lay in East Berlin and Paul couldn't bring himself to go into the Russian sector, fearing that, unlike his mother, he would never get out. He sent his guide through Checkpoint Charlie to see what might be left. The man reported that the old neighborhood had been leveled by bombing and that a People's housing project now covered the area.

His guide was a standoffish, taciturn man, so Paul had barely said a word to anyone since his arrival, except to order food he knew from dining in Yorkville ... wursts and wiener schnitzel mostly.

The one brief conversation he did have discouraged him from seeking more. He was in a coffee bar reading, when he became aware that the man at the next table was pointing at his paperback novel and smiling broadly. "American?" the man asked and when Paul said yes, the man began speaking in lopsided English that Paul had difficulty sorting and, finally, wished he hadn't.

"We have many Americans here. They marched in and stayed. For what? Must be a dreadful expense for your taxpayers to put up with. For what? I ask again. What did we do? I know what you are told. All that nonsense about death camps and eleven million people destroyed. How could that be? I was a little boy during the war, but I remember. It was not like in your movies. Only the rich and well placed were permitted to be Nazis. The rest were like my papa, only soldiers who did what they were told. You go home and tell your people we didn't kill anybody but our enemies, just as you did. Death camps! What nonsense."

The man produced several pamphlets from his pocket, riffled through them, and handed one to Paul, saying, "Here is truth in English. We have this printed in eight languages. It proves there were no death camps. There is an address on back to write for more. Eight languages. We must stop this lie, if we Germans are to regain our dignity and stature in the world."

The man rose, bowed, and scurried away. Paul looked at the pamphlet dubiously, then read it. When he was done, he tore it in half, thinking, "...and the earth is flat, you dumb bastard."

Despite his lack of activity, Paul didn't feel a moment's calm, only the low hum of unidentified agitation. His main concern was becoming that, after nine days, he had already finished twelve of the twenty mystery novels he had brought with him.

On the tenth day he packed, checked out, and went to Tegel Airport to get one of the eighty flights within Germany that came and went daily. He decided on Munich, because it was the first flight out. More than Berlin's buildings had been destroyed, and Paul was happy Leda had never returned to the ruins.

In Munich he checked into a suite at the Vier Jahreszeiten. Before being led upstairs he asked the concierge to find someone to serve as a translator and secretary, but this time specified he wanted someone who had experience in locating people who'd gone missing in the war. The concierge promised to have someone suitable by tomorrow, at whatever time was convenient for the gentleman. The earlier the better, Paul said, and was called an hour later and told that Miss Sybella Walter could come to his suite at ten the next morning.

In the morning he dressed carefully, feeling, for some reason, he should look his best for the interview. Then it occurred to him that being alone with a woman, telling her what he was doing and why, might not be comfortable — might, indeed, be very embarrassing. He had spent no time with any women but his mother, Maria, and his secretary in months. Sex was a vague memory of times past. The idea of being alone with a woman was disquieting.

The doorbell to his suite rang. He opened the door, but turned back into the room immediately, barely glancing at the woman. As they talked, he moved distractedly about the room, as if looking for something lost.

She stood watching him move nervously about and wishing he'd ask her to sit down. She wondered if he was going to be like that terrible Hoffmeier last month who had kept making dashes at her and disarranging her clothes. But that had turned out all right, because she'd finally slapped the man, and he'd wept and given her a raise.

Paul was making her nervous, so she said, "If I've come at a bad time, Mr. Howe, I would be happy to come back later."

Paul stopped, startled by her clear voice and British accent. He stopped pacing, but still didn't look directly at her. "Oh, no," he said. "The time is fine. And please, sit down. Would you like some coffee?"

Without waiting for her answer he called room service and ordered coffee for two. She kept a wary eye on him.

He finally sat, gripping the arms of the chair as if to anchor himself to it.

"I've come to Berlin to look for a friend of my mother's. She lost track of him after she left Berlin in 1935. She died recently and left him a little something. If he's alive I'd like to find him and be sure he gets it."

Sybella wondered what a "little something" was to a man who could afford this suite in this hotel, to say nothing of the airfare, her cost, other expenses.

"I have no idea where to start. That's why I asked the hotel to find me someone with experience."

"I've been of some help to others, but only occasionally. Most times it has been an expensive exercise in futility. You understand that I can make no promises. In fact, we will most likely reach a point where I will feel obliged to suggest we cease. Some people do not like to hear I feel their search has become hopeless. So, I think it best to be clear from the start."

He didn't respond and she went on, "I bill through the hotel by the hour and I have a minimum of four hours a day. Do you speak any German, Mr. Howe?"

"Menu German, and even then I can't get much past bratwurst," Paul said as he answered the knock on the door. A waiter wheeled in a mahogany-and-brass cart with a lavish presentation of coffee that he poured and passed, making a fussy drama of it. Sybella watched with both amusement and irritation, thinking that the cost of their coffee would probably feed her for three days. She hated worrying about money and disliked herself for envying those who had it.

The waiter finished, flourished his napkin over his arm, and bowed himself out.

They sat in self-conscious silence over coffee and took in one another covertly. She found him good-looking enough, and without the gloss of overgroomed wealth she had come to associate with rich Americans. He saw a rather severe-looking woman who wore her hair pulled into a taut knot at the back of her head. Her only makeup was pale pink lipstick, and she looked chunky in a gray tweed suit and white blouse. He was relieved. He found her plainness comforting; her appearance didn't suggest anything but business, which was exactly the effect she tried for. In her business there were too many Hoffmeiers.

"If I might make a couple of suggestions," she ventured. "If your friend was Jewish, there are a remarkable number of search resources." She paused for his answer.

"He wasn't."

"Then the Red Cross in Arolsen is the best alternative."

Paul shook his head. "I've been in touch, but all I had was his last address and name. Even I could see the information was pretty slim. I offered a big donation if they would assign some good people and make it a priority. They said they'd welcome the money, but they probably still wouldn't be able to be of much help."

"Then our best option is to advertise in newspapers every day. We also try to find relatives and visit old neighborhoods, assuming they're still standing."

"My mother's old neighborhood is gone."

"I was speaking of the man's."

Paul felt an embarrassment he knew his mother would have found amusing, but said, "My mother was living with this man." Hastening to explain, he added, "They weren't lovers. She was hiding him. The Nazis were after him. She took care of him until the Nazis caught up with him and then she had to run for her own life. There's a lot more, but I suppose the only other thing you need to know now is that her name was Leda Kohl."

"Like the pianist's."

"She was the pianist."

Sybella looked grave, but all she did was nod and say, "Ah."

"And the man's?"

"Dieter Holtman."

"One *n* or two?"

"One."

"Last address?"

He told her.

"In Berlin?"

He nodded and she continued, "I should point out that advertising can take months and cost a great deal. Considering how long ago it was, there's a good chance the man may be dead, otherwise he might well have been in touch with your mother. She would have been fairly easy to contact, considering how famous she was. I don't mean to be discouraging, just honest about what's involved."

Sybella hated being honest, but could never seem to stop herself. Why couldn't she do what others did and milk the situation?

"I'd suggest we start by preparing an ad for the major newspapers in both the East and West sectors.

She drew a pad from her briefcase and wrote quickly. Within minutes she said, "Something like this, perhaps," and read, "'Seeking Dieter Holtman on behalf of Leda Kohl, pianist, with whom he shared Berlin flat in 1935, prior to his disappearance.'"

She explained, "Box numbers are best for replies, as they keep those who answer at a distance. Do you want to say anything about the bequest? Inheritances draw some charlatans, but money can also attract solid information. I'm quite good at sorting such people out. The greedy tend to be obvious. Can you tell me anything only a reliable source would know about Holtman?

"I don't mean to take command, but since you don't speak German I would have to manage matters, unless they speak English. Also, offering a small reward might help. Not too big, as it draws greedy people who prey on the hopeful."

Her businesslike ability to organize was starting to reassure him. For the first time since beginning his search he felt that his plan might not be as mad as it sometimes felt, that they could discover whether Holtman was alive or dead. For her part, Sybella began to wonder what he was leaving out of his story. Every time he spoke of Holtman, he seemed to be carefully editing his remarks.

They discussed the amount of the reward and she had to talk him down from a figure she found extravagant. They agreed that the reward should be given, whether Holtman was dead or alive. More as a courtesy, as she knew he couldn't read German, she showed him her list of newspapers that still carried the "Seeking Lost Relatives and Friends" ad columns and told him how much each charged for the ad they proposed.

In little more than an hour she gave him a brief course in finding those gone missing in the war. She put her work in her briefcase and rose.

"I think we've covered everything we can today. I have the use of a telephone and typewriter in the hotel, so I'll go down and get started on placing the ads. I'll prepare an agenda for our next meeting."

Actually, she wasn't so much businesslike as starved. She had left home early to be here by ten and she wanted to get away before her stomach started announcing her hunger.

She said, "Here's my card, and I have one of those new call-taking machines," and started to the door.

Paul realized he couldn't stand the idea of eating another meal alone in silence and asked, "I know it's early, but would you like to have lunch with me? Perhaps you could suggest the place."

She looked at him warily and wondered if he wasn't another Hoffmeier. On the other hand, a really splendid lunch would be worth a little sparring. She tried to think of some place with tables wide enough to preclude knee-grabbing, but her memory of the extraordinary Walterspiel restaurant downstairs made her reckless and she suggested they dine there. For the kind of food they served, let him grab.

As they entered the restaurant the maitre d' greeted them and said in German to Sybella, "How nice to see you again, Mrs. Tanzer. It's been a long time. We've missed you." She saw the maitre d' assess her unstylish appearance and could almost hear him think, "Things have certainly changed for you, Mrs. Tanzer."

How long had it been since she'd dined here? Four years? She had missed it, as she sometimes did beautiful clothes and charming, if fleeting, friends. She had not missed that bastard Tanzer. Since Tanzer, she'd made a life that suited her, and regarded her past with the rueful detachment of an older person for a hopelessly young friend who'd made a fool of herself.

She pored over the menu the way devout Christians regard Gutenberg Bibles. It promised glories. Tanzer had never allowed her the full play of her love for food, saying he loathed fat women and it wouldn't do for a man in his position to have an unsightly wife. Despite the fact that she never gained an ounce, he had convinced her that obesity could strike overnight.

Being married to the stage star Otto Tanzer had been publicly enviable and privately messy, starting with their honeymoon in Cairo where he was doing two weeks' work playing General Rommel in a television movie about World War II. She hadn't been so much dismayed by his chasing the women of the company – not even when he caught them – as embarrassed by his lack of pretense. She had also been under the impression she was his third wife. She found she had the dubious distinction of being his fifth. Her self-assurance slipped further when she overheard a member of the cast say of her, Otto's latest bride, "Marriage is Otto's way of saying goodbye."

Not that she had married Otto in the blush of first love. She'd had entirely too much flaming passion with Klaus and, ardor spent, had found herself poorer in spirit and purse. Following the sexual festival of Klaus, her peasant practicality had reasserted itself and she made up her mind that her next affair would be tempered by such earthy considerations as marriage, the man's income, and his career. She had met Otto Tanzer backstage at the experimental theatre where she worked as their costume designer. Tanzer had come backstage one night trailing his fame and cashmere coat, strewing fulsome praise to one and all for their Absurdist production of Schiller. When Otto turned and saw her, she felt like a rabbit eyeing oncoming headlights and did what rabbits do, sat and accepted the inevitable.

Otto was a first-class wooer and she decided that the rough justice of sexual law had earned her an Otto, because of what she had suffered with Klaus.

When she was sure Otto was serious — and Otto was never less than *serious* — she put self-interest first and ignored the tales of Otto's previous wives and gossip about his amatory profligacy.

This time around the "production quality" of her life was classy, with good clothes, fine restaurants, an impressive address, and position among the best people of theatre and society. What she hadn't anticipated was the constant nursing his ego would require.

She ran a one-patient intensive care ward for his fragile ego. She bandaged the wounds inflicted by bad actresses, insensitive directors, and rotten lighting, until she started wondering whether the other women in Otto's life couldn't do some of the custodial work. She even talked to one of Otto's mistresses and found that when he was with the woman, he was all charm, consideration, generosity, and good cheer. Her resentment and shopping increased.

As with all his wives, Otto began to feel that, for what he was spending on her, he wasn't getting nearly enough value for his money. But, by then, they were both so weary of one another that the best either could summon was a halfhearted snarl or weary look of disgust. She began to see less of him, and he saw more of his mistresses.

They might have limped on this way, if it hadn't been for Otto's current diversion, Clara.

Otto arrived at Clara's ready to shower and put on the tuxedo he kept there. He was in the mood for a gala evening, but he found Clara sullen, accusatory, and very drunk. He tried gaiety and ebullience, kissing and nakedness to wheedle her out of her mood, but she was determined to stay in her funk. "You're never going to leave that woman to marry me," Clara screamed. Otto knew that, but didn't like it being spoken of. Men of his stature didn't marry salesgirls. He took her drink from her, poured it and the rest of the bottle down the toilet, and got into the shower. Quiet firmness was called for.

Dry, dressed, and reassured by his mirror that he was a handsome devil, he left the bedroom. If she wasn't dressed, he would go to the party without her. He found her in the kitchen with a fresh bottle.

"Leave!" she screamed. *"I'm* going to. All I do is sit here and get older, waiting for the Master to show up and throw one to me with that nasty little bratwurst I can barely find under that belly. Some leading man! You should be playing Father Time." With unerring aim she went on to hit his every uncertainty as a man and actor.

He downed a large drink and stormed out, feeling cheated of money, sex, and a good party. He was now in no mood for a party. What he needed was wifely soothing. He walked home to clear his head, and with an actor's imagination recast himself en route. Sybella wasn't so bad and maybe it was time to settle down, assume a more mature role, have children, play the paterfamilias. Indeed, it might well be time to move on to more mature parts, onstage as well as off.

He arrived home to find Sybella watching television. He told Sybella he had to talk to her and unknotted his black bow tie to add a note of casualness to his costume.

In the voice he used for close-ups, he told Sybella he had been thinking, that they should both try to make this a real marriage. As he spoke he warmed to the role, borrowing lines from old scripts. Needing a good finish line, he improvised, "I want us to have children," and Sybella started to laugh. For the second time in three hours, Otto's dignity felt a deep wound and, worse, he knew how badly he'd played against type.

When Sybella could stop laughing, she said, "Oh, for God's sake, Otto, what makes you think I'd have a baby's baby?" and started to laugh again. Otto struck her and she collapsed back in her chair.

He stormed off to catch the end of his party and find a sympathetic ear. Sybella spent the rest of the evening destroying his prized wardrobe. She couldn't find the kitchen scissors, so she tried her nail scissors which were useless against the sturdy fabrics. So she heaped his clothes in the tub and poured nail polish, detergents, shampoo, perfume, and any destructive kitchen liquid she could find on the lot. It made a satisfying stench and a lot of suds.

Although her attorneys begged her to play the abused neglected wife, she showed such disdain for Otto that the judge saw her as a harpy. Besides, hadn't the judge heard it rumored that Otto kept many mistresses content and well tended? Sybella received a flat amount in settlement that was soon gone, because she'd forgotten how to live within her means.

When she was almost out of money, she awoke to find herself thirty-one, low on funds, and with six years of her life gone. She saw deeper laugh lines she knew she hadn't gotten with Otto, and crow's-feet made, she thought, by a very large crow.

She didn't want to go back to theatre work, so she restored her secretarial skills and built a sturdy business with the patrons of the better hotels in Munich. She had made a life that was safe and too often felt entirely too sedate.

Now, here she sat with Mr. Howe in the lovely Walterspiel devouring several courses with dedication.

"You must have been very hungry," Paul said as he watched her finish an assault on a raspberry tart.

"Starved," she said. "I live fairly far out, so I had an early breakfast. I know that ladies aren't supposed to eat like ditch-diggers, but I don't put on weight. I hate the idea that I might have to diet someday."

He told her he envied her pleasure in food. She hadn't said much during the meal, but he was too pleased at having a companion for lunch to care.

He said, "There's something else you might be able to help me with. I don't have a driver's license and I'd like to see something of Bavaria. I don't want a limousine, because people are always staring in. Could you recommend someone?"

As it was off-season and he was her only client at the moment, she said, "I could drive you. I would have to bill a little more for my time, but that would include the use of my car, of course. Just tell me what you want to see, or, if you like, I could work out an itinerary."

"That would be fine," he said, and smiled for the first time.

She smiled back and prayed, Please, God, not another Hoffmeier. On the other hand, he's not bad-looking and I'm not the Primavera. Fact is, I'm at the slippery end of thirty. A grab or two might be rather nice.

≀

Sybella took full command of finding Dieter. She called friends in Berlin to see whether Leda's old neighborhood was indeed gone or if the man Paul had used in Berlin had taken the money without bothering to go look. She found the man had told the truth. The newspaper ads elicited a dozen vague and unhelpful replies that showed more interest in the reward than in providing facts, but she followed up each to its dead end.

Only one letter with a Munich postmark seemed in the least promising. Sybella wrote "M. Fuchs" twice, trying to get specifics, but the replies remained intriguingly vague. Finally, a meeting was arranged at the Max-Joseph Platz, a large open public area in front of the National Theatre not far from Paul's hotel.

Sybella explained their strategy. "We carry no bags or briefcases. Too easy to steal, if M. Fuchs is actually a team of thieves. You wear a money belt with the reward to protect against their luring you there to pick your pocket. They work in pairs, sometimes threes. One bumps or distracts you and the other plucks you clean."

"How do you know all this?"

"Hard experience."

They arrived on time and waited for half an hour. No one approached them. Only one young man loitered nearby, obviously appraising them. He finally moved off. They never heard from M. Fuchs again. No other likely letters arrived, but Paul made no plans to return to New York. He found he liked Munich and liked Sybella's company.

He came quickly to depend on her and, no matter what needed doing, she seemed able to get it done with dispatch. His lack of German made him uneasy with salespeople, and she would move slightly ahead of him to the counter and tell the salesperson what was needed – socks, a sweater when the weather turned unseasonably cold, shaving cream, blades. In restaurants she described unfamiliar dishes in detail – *gebratener Hummer, gebackene Seezunge, Leipziger Allerlei* – that turned out to be nothing more exotic than fried lobster, deep-fried sole, and mixed vegetables. She proved an expert guide and tutor, and he quickly learned Munich's byways and even tried pronouncing the tongue-numbing street names. His pronunciation often landed far off the mark, but he earned her praise for trying and got a little better.

When, after three weeks of being together, Paul hadn't yet made a pass, Sybella began to relax and dress more casually and attractively, not to stir his interest, but because she remembered she liked looking attractive and hadn't given a damn for a very long time. She thought his platonic attitude might have one of any number of causes: he might be impotent or gay, or she might have slipped beyond being the kind of woman that men her own age made passes at. That she had moved beyond being desirable and that it had happened without her noticing, gave her only fleeting discomfort. If she had, well, too bad. She was coming to enjoy him and, besides, sex and love had never brought her anything but mess. It would be nice to simply enjoy a man as a friend.

He found her companionable. Yes, that was the word — companionable. Perhaps being her employer created a neutral ground. He noticed as her clothes became gradually more attractive and was pleased by the effect. Conversation now passed easily between them, but they had yet to venture into any personal areas.

Near his fourth weekend in Munich he suggested they take the long drive north to see Herne, where his mother had grown up. The trip would require staying overnight, so she booked rooms — for him their best suite, for herself a modest single — and they left on a Friday at five a.m. This time he was sure that, unlike Berlin, he would have some sense of knowing the town, feel some emotional link to the past. What he found was a small city newly built after massive wartime bombing. The air strikes of the Allies had shattered even this fairly obscure city of a hundred thousand or so. The rebuilt Herne had a scoured look and was rigorously spare of line, as if determined to not be the least bit interesting. People moved busily about, but it felt like a movie set where everyone had been hired to create the illusion of occupation.

They dined in the hotel's restaurant, knowing it would probably be dreary, but the other restaurants they looked into didn't appear any more promising. Over dinner he told her what little he knew of his mother's childhood there, of her memories of the coming of the Nazis, of his grandparents' death in an air raid.

"My mother would never return after the war, not even to play one concert. Maybe she felt that the fate she'd escaped would overtake her if she did. She never even spoke German again, except for her more colorful cursing."

"Do you miss her?" Sybella asked.

"Every day. Those last months she became one of the best friends I've ever had."

"What a nice memory to have. My mother still thinks I'm six years old. Sometimes I am. She's had it hard. She always had to work to keep us going and it wasn't easy, especially after the war. My grandfather was killed in the First World War and my father died in the Second. They seemed to be around only long enough to start families."

Over coffee she said, apropos of nothing, "I'm almost forty," and he said, "That's nice. I mean I don't think I'd be as comfortable with you otherwise." She smiled in answer, having no idea how to take his remark.

They said good night on the elevator and went to their rooms. In front of her mirror she examined her face with unusual intentness and scrutinized its condition, then slathered on more night cream. He lay naked on his thick down mattress, hating its billowy softness and feeling the first poignant twinge of loneliness he had allowed himself in longer than he could remember. The feeling made him restless.

He got up, dressed, and went out into ten-o'clock-empty streets. He wandered through seemingly endless rows of new buildings on streets lit by glacial light. Every so often he stopped to peer up blank streets that seemed no different from the one he was on. Changing direction was like walking into a mirror. The whoosh and rumble of far-off automobiles on an autobahn accentuated the silent emptiness. He knew there were people, because windows flickered with bluish light from television sets.

He lost track of where he was and began turning in circles at a corner, hoping to spy some landmark. Well, he wasn't sleepy, so if he wandered lost it didn't make a lot of difference. He'd probably come across a cabstand. He walked toward some shop windows, and, in the display of a record store, he found the ghost he'd been seeking, for behind the glass was a large picture of his mother on a poster for DDG Records. Around the poster were album covers of Leda's records, the jackets chronicling her from a fresh, dark-haired young woman in her twenties with an open candid expression of delight, to a woman in her fifties with wings of champagne-colored hair framing a face of remarkable intelligence and self-containment. A hand-lettered sign in German stood among the album covers, but all he could read of it was his mother's name. He stared at the sign's meaningless message and felt a desperate need to know what it said.

Suddenly, the tears he hadn't cried since his mother's death came.

He didn't hear the police car pull up or hear the two officers until they were on either side of him. One of them addressed him in German and Paul stared blankly. Then they each spoke in turn, further addling him. Had he broken a law? Or was Herne like Los Angeles, where lone walkers were suspect?

The officers eyed him oddly and began to feel tense about this stranger who seemed so agitated, perhaps drugged. Finally, one said in clumsy English, "American?" Paul nodded and they relaxed, apparently feeling that the condition of being American explained odd behavior.

Paul pointed into the window and said, "My mother," then recalled the German: *"Mutter."* Seeing their baffled look he ventured uncertainly, *"Mein Mutter,"* and pointed from the poster to himself, repeating, *"Mein Mutter. Mein Mutter."* Then both began to talk to him at once, smiling and bobbing their heads, apparently understanding and obviously full of approval. As they started away, he stopped them and tried several pronunciations of his hotel's name, until he remembered the hotel's matchbook in his pocket and showed it to them. They put him in the backseat and delivered him to his door. They bowed him out of their car, one miming playing a piano and repeating, *"Mutter.* Leda Kohl, Leda Kohl. *Ja, ja."*

The next morning he had Sybella ask at the desk about nearby record shops and they walked to three others before he found the one with his mother's records in the window. She translated the sign for him:

"We are proud to carry every existing recording made by Leda Kohl, the preeminent interpreter of German composers who was born and began her long and distinguished career in Herne, and who remains this city's finest and proudest contribution to world music."

Sybella said, "This must make you feel very proud," and he asked, "I wonder how it would have made my mother feel?" then answered his own question: "Very proud, I think."

They drove back to Munich that afternoon and he felt content, sure that the trip to Herne had been worth the effort.

❧

Only three more letters came in the next three weeks in answer to the ads that were still running. These were more obviously bogus than most. There was nothing to keep him in Munich, but he stayed and it was soon early June. He and Sybella toured museums, lunched, went to Schloss Nymphenburg twice, and saw something of the countryside. She turned down two customers at other hotels to remain available to Paul, but began to feel uncomfortable about charging him for what felt like a holiday. She wanted to be businesslike with him, but couldn't figure out how to do it without giving the impression that she didn't want to be with him or wasn't having a perfectly fine time.

For all they saw, there was no sign that a war had ravaged this city. He asked Sybella and she pointed out that thirty years had passed since the war ended, a generation and a half. She said that all that remained was Dachau, the Holocaust memorial they could visit, if he wanted.

Sybella organized the day's outing. Unsure of where they might dine nearby, she packed a picnic lunch of sandwiches which she made gala with a split of champagne, a tiny jar of caviar, and slices of *Linzertorte*. They had splendid weather that put them in wonderful spirits as they drove the twenty miles to Dachau.

Tall, rickety wooden guard towers were the first things they saw as they walked from the parking lot toward Dachau's entrance. The towers were jerry-built wooden boxes on stilts that, because of their apparent fragility, looked anything but threatening. Above the main entrance was a sign in German that Sybella translated for him as "Work Makes Freedom." They entered, passing two barbed-wire fences, one fence within the other, meant to double the difficulty of escape.

They joined their English-speaking tour group and the woman guide marched them off smartly. Paul noticed that, unlike most tours he had been on, the people on this one tended to cluster more closely together, although there was nothing visibly ominous in the blank-faced, white one-story buildings that lined the broad unpaved dirt avenue leading from the gates. The soberly dressed guide spoke in a loud and precise voice:

"Dachau was a model camp founded in 1933 to which Red Cross officials were brought to show the humane conditions in which Nazi internees were kept."

Paul saw only one child in the group and was startled by the mother's hysterical reaction when the boy darted toward one of the deserted dormitories. She swept after him and seized him up roughly, a look of horror on her face, as if the boy had been racing toward an onrushing truck. She gripped the child so tightly that he whimpered and squirmed in pain.

"Built to house only hundreds, thousands were often interned here, necessitating ways of exterminating the excess population."

Paul lost track of what the guide was saying. To him, the camp didn't look much worse than an army training barracks and it looked better to him than pictures he had seen of housing for migrant workers. The guide led them into a building in which rough-hewn three-tier bunks were crammed together.

"...crowding necessitated three people to a bunk bed barely wide enough for one."

Paul watched a woman surreptitiously pry a sliver of wood from the edge of a bunk. She saw Paul staring at her and hurried off guiltily with her souvenir. Sybella smiled at him, shook her head, and said, "People."

"The toll in human life among the three hundred camps throughout Nazi-occupied Europe was eleven million: six million Jews, the other five million were politicals, criminals, anti-socials, Jehovah's Witnesses, emigrants, homosexuals, and Gypsies, each person identified by one or more of the thirty-two triangular fabric badges of different colors and varied design."

They wandered up and down featureless dusty alleys between the buildings as their guide droned on, and Paul found himself losing interest and wondering whether they were now farther from the entrance or the exit. He wanted to leave. He looked at his shoes and found to his irritation that they were gray with dust. The group plodded on in a huddle and Paul began to feel cheated: there was no war here, no signs of battle or contest, no devastation, just acres of empty boring buildings sanitized of human experience.

"The building immediately ahead was the camp's brothel, staffed normally with Jewish women and used to discourage homosexuality and provide a normal outlet for favored prisoners and guards alike."

Ahead he saw a new building with signs in several languages announcing Dachau's museum and Paul hoped that this was the end and craned his neck for the sight of an exit. He took Sybella's hand to help her through the museum's door. The contrast between the brilliant sun and this darkened interior momentarily blinded them and they stood still, uncertain of their footing. All he could see clearly were the artistically lit exhibits and photographic blowups. Paul led Sybella aside and stood holding her hand. The guide noticed that they had slipped from the group and said sternly, "If you would please stay together. There is another group immediately behind us that is not English-speaking." Paul and Sybella edged obediently back.

"This exhibit contains the artifacts of the camp ... the crafts work of the prisoners, their uniforms with their vertical stripes in black and white, and photographs taken by the SS."

Paul moved with Sybella toward an immense blowup of the street on which they had entered, but in the picture the street was not deserted – it was clogged with men and only men. The prisoners leaned from windows, they stood about aimlessly, apparently shy of the cameraman. Not one of them was talking with another. Everyone's attention was fixed on the photographer and there seemed to be a question on every face. Paul imagined himself as the photographer who must have been on a ladder or atop a truck. For the photographer it would have been just another job, like photographing a general's wedding or a medal-pinning ceremony. His height above the mass lent distance, showed he had nothing to do with this rabble, these enemies of his fine new triumphant order.

The men's expressions seemed to ask, "Why is he taking our picture? Where will this picture be seen and by whom? Does this photographer represent some new innovation in terror?" The effect was to make the men look furtive with their hollowed ashen faces, and starting eyes that seemed as unnaturally large as a baby's.

Paul tried to imagine sound but couldn't. He tried to imagine colors − skin tones, blue sky, the yellowish earth of the street − but he couldn't summon any. He saw only colorless faces and black-and-white uniforms against raw wood buildings under an overcast sky. The only color would have been their badges ... red, blue, orange, green, yellow, pink. Paul began to examine the picture for details, and noted the dirty hands and the lank hair, the missing teeth in slack mouths. And there were no guards in sight, which made it seem as if this were some remarkable community of criminals who had imprisoned themselves voluntarily and remained there, not from duress, but from guilt.

His gaze fixed on one man and the inverted triangle Paul could see on his trouser leg. Paul looked at the face and beneath its hungry uncertainty he could glimpse how young the man was, young enough to be his son. The face seemed so intent that Paul feared the man was about to say something, but not something terrible, not a cry of pain or a plea for help; he was sure the man was about to offer him a blessing, to tell him something about love and Paul leaned toward the picture's whispered message.

Sybella was gripping his trembling arm and asking, "Paul, what's the matter? Are you ill? Come outside."

He was shaking so badly that his legs wouldn't work and he said softly, "What if that's Dieter?" and his imagination rampaged, throwing up images of this man as his father, of his pregnant mother running up a street from a woman who brandished a lettuce and screamed that the whore would be punished. And, most terrible, he had a vision of himself as some half-human thing in his mother's womb.

A tourist saw Sybella's difficulty and took Paul's other arm. Between them they guided him outside where he stood rigidly, both hands folded over his eyes as if to block the high sun and not the picture that had burned into his mind.

The man who had helped them said, "This place has that effect on some people who've lost relatives here. They can't help but think, 'What if that had been me?'"

Paul didn't hear what he said, but Sybella replied that it might just be heat or hunger and led him to their car.

On the drive back to Munich, Paul told Sybella the whole story of Leda and Dieter. He put down the burden of his secret and felt the first peace he'd known in months.

When they reached the hotel, Paul said, "Now I'm starved and I'll bet you could eat a horse."

"Just have it led in."

They ate in the Walterspiel and, as if it were in the normal course of their lives, went up to Paul's suite and undressed one another. They spent a long leisurely time exploring one another, then Paul moved to lie on top of her and fell out of bed. He lay on the floor laughing in surprise, Sybella leaning over and watching him.

She asked, "You coming back up or should I come down?"

"Why don't you come down. It's been so long since I've done this that I obviously don't know how to do it on a bed."

They made love twice, then Paul ordered champagne.

{

As they sipped champagne on the bed, both naked, Paul told himself that what he was feeling was probably too great a leap beyond good sense. He remembered a navy buddy's line about building the Taj Mahal around one fuck. For her part, Sybella fretted about billing. What part of the day should she bill him for? She could hardly bill for the whole day without feeling she'd changed professions.

Her confusion grew worse as the next fews days passed. What was business and what pleasure? One morning they worked for an hour and then he took her to Lederer and insisted on buying her an expensive handbag. She grew less sure of where work ended and pleasure began, as she enjoyed her time with him. Still, she needed to make a living.

Paul started thinking of his life in New York and was surprised to find there was less to think about than seemed possible. Were his only ties to New York his office and his new unfurnished apartment? Sad to say, yes. Everything of importance could be handled by letters and phone calls. He thought, There's something to carve on my tombstone: He did it all long-distance.

He wondered what Leda would do and knew. She'd say, Why not? Well, if he made a damned fool of himself, so what? Years of caution had left him with so little.

Several days passed in sex, shopping, some work for his business, and eating. In fleeting moments she stewed about paying her rent and he pondered how to just give her money without offending her. Neither remembered Dieter Holtman until one morning when they returned from lunch and were given a letter forwarded by one of the Berlin newspapers they'd been advertising in. It was the first in three weeks. They took it upstairs, threw it on the desk, and themselves on the bed. Twenty-odd bogus letters had taught them not to be hopeful.

Later, Sybella put on one of Paul's shirts and took the letter near the window. The cheap envelope bore an East Berlin postmark and dirty smudges. Sybella said, "It looks as if someone kicked it here from Berlin."

She began to read and grew more still and intent as she did. Then she read it again, squinting at it, as if trying to see between the lines. She finally said, "My God, I think this is genuine, Paul.

"I'll have to translate as I go, so bear with me. 'To the person who placed the ad in the *Berlin Zeitung:* I knew Dieter Holtman in the Flossenbürg concentration camp where he was from 1941 through 1945. He was twenty-seven years old when I met him and a somewhat ... a fairly ... tall man who often spoke of Leda Kohl and of being familiar ... knowing ... her in Berlin. He knew she was alive, because he heard one of her records on an illegal radio a prisoner had built. She had gone ... run away ... to America. He told me that when he first met her he was playing piano in a Berlin club called the Blue Wink. He said he often played Jewish-American composers to fox the Nazis, a foolish thing for him to do. People like him should not have drawn attention to themselves. He also made a living at that time by sewing dresses for men who indulged in that kind of vice.' He uses a more pejorative word, Paul, but that's close enough.

"Let's see ... He goes on, 'Dieter said he had no relatives, so I can only imagine that the person looking is Leda Kohl or that brother of hers Dieter mentioned. If you are Leda Kohl you are in a position to present ... offer ... a reward that would make it worth my while to place myself in some danger to tell you more. Your advertisement does not specific ... specify ... an amount, but I would need five thousand American dollars to make it worth the personal risk I would undertake ... assume ... in meeting with you or telling you more. I am late in answering, because it is not within my means to buy a daily paper and I read only back issues I find. This should tell you that I am in need of the reward. Naturally, if it was within my ability to give such information for free, I would naturally do so. If this is ... agreeable ... you may write *poste restante* to me in Berlin.' It's signed 'Horst Kleber.'"

"The letter's real," Paul said. "When is it dated?"

"Last Saturday, postmarked East Berlin. I should tell you that I've cleaned up his grammar and his spelling is awful. He's not educated."

"I can't believe it. I went through the motions, but they never seemed quite real. That letter's real. But he doesn't say what happened, if Holtman's alive."

"That's what the five thousand is for."

"So, he's uneducated but shrewd. What's the fastest way to get a letter back to him? The five thousand is fine, but only if he has information on what happened to Dieter after the war. Tell him that's all I'll pay the full amount for. If Holtman's alive, where is he? If he's dead, I want to know where he's buried and verify it.

"It's Tuesday. If he had our letter by Friday we should hear ... when? ... Monday or Tuesday? Tell him that if we meet I will have to bring a translator with me, because I don't speak German. We don't want to spook him with a surprise guest."

Then he added in a tone he hoped made the idea sound like a spontaneous afterthought, "As long as I may be here for a while longer, let's go rent me an apartment."

The furnished apartment they found for him was in Munich's stylish Schwabing district, a bohemian area adjacent to the large and beautiful park, the English Garden. The apartment was small and comfortable and looked across a pedestrian mall toward a similar building across the way that housed a popular pastry shop with a sidewalk cafe.

It took him two days to convince her to move in with him, and, for her part, she didn't so much make a decision as close her eyes and leap.

Two weeks later, Kleber wrote again and claimed to know Dieter Holtman's whereabouts. It took two more weeks of dealing with Kleber's needlessly complicated negotiations, before a time and place to meet were set.

The plan worried Sybella, and Paul dreaded the coming encounter in East Berlin for other reasons. Sybella feared smuggling five thousand American dollars into East Berlin, where dealing in Western currencies was harshly punished. Kleber must know that, or was that part of the greedy man's plan?

⸙

Paul felt like an archeologist burrowing into past ages. With every block they passed the buildings got older and more dilapidated, the streets shabbier and more pitted, the shops poorer, the people more ill-clad. Sybella and he were moving deep into the Communist sector of East Berlin that the bombs had missed and postwar life had bypassed. The buildings they saw had never been solid, nor built to be anything more than places to keep the working poor roughly housed. The people matched the sad architecture, wearing clothes and expressions that spoke of lives without hope of improvement.

Sybella was anxious and wary, and told Paul it might not do for him to be heard speaking English. They walked in silence and began to speak only when they reached an area where no one was to be seen on the street.

He said, "I didn't think East Berlin had neighborhoods like this. It's so bleak. I thought Communist states took care of everything, like Sweden."

"That's why I'm so scared about carrying all this money. We shouldn't have agreed to bring American dollars. What if

–158–

there's a big reward for turning in currency smugglers? This man could be anyone, and in this kind of neighborhood people turn their backs on trouble."

She stopped. "We're there," Sybella said, pointing up at a street sign precariously bolted to a brick building. They peered down a dirty dead-end alley full of trash cans and litter. The doorways and grimy windows on either side were only a few feet apart, forcing unwanted intimacy on the tenants.

"It looks like an abandoned warehouse. It's depressing," Paul said. "If he was with Holtman in the camps, how did he end up here? I thought the internees from the camps got some kind of indemnity and pension from the government."

"Most do. Paul, I'm very nervous. It feels all wrong."

Yes, it did, but he didn't say so, just took her hand to lead her along the deserted alley toward number 11. He said, "I'm thinking how much more scared I'd be if you weren't with me. I hope your karate's as good as you said it was."

"American men are supposed to be able to handle any emergency. What kind of American are you?"

"The cowardly urban kind." They stood in front of number 11 and regarded dubiously the distempered acid green paint on the windowless door and a scrawled number that spoke of its tentative hope that anyone might seek it out. There was no bell. He pulled her to him protectively and put his hand against the door and pushed, saying, "Well, here goes."

Just inside, they found the nameplate of "H. Kleber" beneath "35" and began the climb up the ramshackle stairs to the fourth floor, crunching through freshly fallen plaster. They passed the open doors to the toilets that served each floor and felt queasy at what they saw. They heard a baby wailing and its cry was the resigned sound of someone who expected no help to come.

As they paused in front of 35, the door was immediately cracked open. They heard a rustling within, someone squinted out, and then the door was pulled swiftly open. The open door exhaled a warmly damp breath of cheap cigarettes and cheaper liquor, old bacon grease, aged varnish, and decades of airless occupancy. The man inside matched; he slouched against the wall, a personification of Sullenness. He was bulky and unkempt and looked, from the tufts of hair that spiked from his scalp, as if he barbered himself. His growth of whiskers might have been the start of a beard. He was somewhat difficult to see in the half-light from the hall, but the impression was disagreeable enough to keep Paul from closer examination and to stall him from entering as Kleber signaled them in. Paul averted his eyes, but he could feel the man's brooding look. Kleber said something in German that came out on a long sigh.

"What?" Paul asked.

"He said, 'So much like Dieter.'"

Paul said, "How the hell can he tell in the dark?"

The man spoke urgently and Sybella translated, "He says we should go in before we're seen."

They passed in, edging past the man and his smell. The door slammed and they heard the noisy clatter of locks closing them in.

Now secure, Kleber broke into a torrent of hospitality, but Paul didn't ask for a translation. They were ushered in with elaborate gestures and motioned toward exhausted armchairs covered with stained blankets, the arm and head areas greasily slick. Paul and Sybella hesitated, then sat.

Kleber addressed Sybella, asking a question with a broadly theatrical courtesy that almost made Sybella laugh. Kleber wasn't looking at her, but was intent on Paul's reactions to Sybella's translations, slyly eager to see if Paul understood German.

"He wants to know if you would like tea or schnapps. He got tea specially for us."

Paul said he wanted neither, and before Sybella could translate, Kleber turned away and sat in a lumpy upholstered chair next to a small table shedding its last varnish. On it stood an unlabeled bottle of schnapps and a half-full glass. They sat almost knee to knee.

Leading from their chairs in the center of the room, aisles ran between stacks of old crumbling cardboard boxes. Some were disintegrating and others bore scabrous black patches of mildew which had dried. Sybella thought, Even mildew can't survive here. Some boxes that had once held liquids had leaked, but that must have been years ago. Sybella wondered what they now held, but no labels or writing suggested their contents. Paul saw that the aisle to his left ran to another room, its doorway draped with a cheap colorless cloth pinned up carelessly. Sybella's nose and throat tried to close against the smell, for everything exhaled deathly neglect. It was impossible to see the size of the room, as its edges disappeared in darkness. It was only the resonance of their voices that revealed how very large it must be.

The only light seeped through a single small window and seemed dim and exhausted by the effort of getting in. Kleber's face was pallid, with only daubs of gray and black to show where his features were. Sybella watched him and thought she probably wouldn't recognize him if she saw him outside this room. His voice belied his bulk; it was light and high, with the edge of a wheedling child's whine.

Sybella spoke at length in German and then turned to Paul: "I've told him I'll translate for you as he speaks and that if he can tell us how to find Dieter Holtman he'll get the money, but not until. He wants to know if we have it on us. I told him we've made careful arrangements for him to get it. He doesn't like that."

The man barked something and Sybella answered irritatedly. She said to Paul, "He wants to know who you are and I told him it wasn't necessary for him to know. He says you look like Dieter. He wants to know if you're related."

"It's none of his business. Tell him so."

Kleber and Sybella exchanged several abruptly short sentences, before Sybella said, "He would like to tell you something about his time with Dieter Holtman, if you would like to hear. He says he wants you to get your money's worth. I think he meant that to be funny."

"Tell him I'd like to know."

There was a further exchange and then Sybella began to translate, stumblingly at first: "He says he comes from Essen. His family was very poor, even before the Great Depression in the twenties. When the Depression came we ... they ... were hungry all the time. Not having enough to eat changes your mind about everything. Then comes − came − inflation.

"He wants to know if you ever saw the picture of a woman with a wheelbarrow full of money she was taking to buy a loaf of bread."

"Tell him no, and ask him what that's got to do with Dieter?"

Sybella translated, then passed back the impatient reply: "He says it has everything to do with his story. He also says he heard Americans were impatient."

Paul sighed. "Tell him to go ahead."

"'My father was a fine machinist. He taught me. But for what? There was no work. It's hard for a young man to not have work or clothes or money for a girlfriend. But everyone wasn't poor and hungry. I never saw a poor hungry Jew.'"

Sybella sat back, closed her eyes, and tried to let his words slip through her, making no effort in her translation to catch Kleber's self-pitying tone or to edit, but merely to be his medium.

"'I was the oldest. There were five children younger than me, two with tuberculosis. My mother hung herself in our

−162−

kitchen when my sister took to the streets to get us money for food. My sister was eleven. Her friends did it. Little boys too. She left my father and me – just a kid myself – to look after the others. All of us jammed in two rooms. My father joined the Brown Shirts, the SA. Not many of them to start, but when good Germans saw how much these men got done, they grew fast. Broke a few heads, pushed in where they weren't wanted, but they got to where the money and help was. The Nazis thought a man had a right to be a man, should be able to feed his family. The Brown Shirts were the only ones willing to fight for what we needed. Goddamned politicians just said boo-hoo and gabbed. As soon as I was old enough, I joined too. They said they could change things and they did. They gave us work, food, and pride.

"'My father was a smart man and he did well with them. Then, Jesus Christ, there was all that shitty business in thirty-four about the faggots running the Brown Shirts. The faggots dishonored good men, real men. They got rid of the faggots, but they'd got their shit on all of us. They knew my father was all right, but the SA was never the same again, not the same pride.

"'When I was old enough I got into the SS and I had enough to get engaged. Dumb girl. I didn't much like her, but the faggots had given SAs a bad name and it made sense to get a wife quick – even one you didn't much care about.'"

Paul spoke to Sybella, who told Kleber that Paul was only interested in what had happened in Flossenbürg concentration camp and how he came to know Dieter. Kleber looked disgusted. He spoke and Sybella translated: "'Nobody wants to hear the truth, to hear why we had to have the Nazis.'"

Kleber poured another drink, and started over with a disdain that Paul could sense even in Sybella's translation: "'Americans don't like to hear about what forced us to do what we did. We were fighting for our lives, for food. Americans don't want to hear that. They want us to grovel and say how wrong we were for what happened. They sit on their fat asses in America telling the world how to be good. And how long would *they* sit and watch the Jews take the food from *their* mouths? How do *they* like the faggots corrupting *their* children? How many of you Americans wish they had the courage to do what we did and get rid of the trash?'"

He went on, but Sybella stopped.

Kleber said angrily to Sybella, "Why aren't you translating?"

It took great restraint for Sybella to say merely, "Mr. Howe wants to know about Herr Holtman. He's familiar with German history."

"Like the Americans say the history is? Well, it's your money. Holtman was a faggot. Just another faggot. You're sure you wouldn't like a drink?"

"No," she said.

"Sorry that I'm out of champagne, madame. Anyway ... Your Dieter was a pansy, but he had his wits about him and he wasn't as scrawny as the rest. Even after all those years in the camps. He'd been in for six years when I met him in Flossenbürg camp over near the Czech border. Dieter was an old hand by the time I was assigned there."

"You were SS?" Sybella asked.

"You think I was one of the shitty trash they kept locked up?"

Sybella raced to catch up with her translation and Paul fixed his attention on Kleber at the mention of Dieter's name.

"Dieter was a pretty boy. Like that one must have been," Kleber said, dipping his head toward Paul. "I wouldn't have bothered with the faggot if they'd given us the brothel they promised. Our commandant was a prude. Didn't get a brothel till near the end of the war, so we had to make do with the fairies. No secret. Everybody winked at it. They expected us to pick out one of the pink triangles, get some good out of the pansies.

"The SS got the choice ones. Even the *Kapos* had to give up their private bum boys if we wanted them. That's the way it worked in the camp. We were the bosses. The *Kapos* were useful and they knew how to keep the scum in line, but they were scum too. Most of the *Kapos* were jailbirds, usually the violent ones, but they were the best for running the work details. Tough, no-shit guys. But not as tough as we were.

"I saw Dieter and thought, That one will do. Good soft ass. Some meat left on him."

Sybella didn't wince, but Kleber said, "Pardon the language, lady, but that's the way it was. Why'd he bring a woman anyway? Did he expect to hear how the flowers grew in Flossenbürg?"

Sybella didn't translate and regarded Kleber impassively.

"Pretty ass on Dieter. Got me all hot. Got me hard as a nun's knees. He was the boyfriend of one of the toughest *Kapos* in Flossenbürg, so he'd been fed. Not too much, you understand. It didn't do for that lot to look too well fed. Caused bad feelings. And his *Kapo* got him soap, so he was clean, too. Most were stinking scarecrows, just these knobby joints and all stringy, and the ladies' tits hung down to their twats. So I bought Dieter from his *Kapo*. For gold. I could have had him for nothing, but fair's fair. Besides, you never knew what shit those *Kapos* would try if you got their bowels grinding.

"If you had a boy you took care of him. That's the way it worked. Extra food, soap, better clothes, easier work, no stone quarry work for your bum boy. I did a lot for Dieter and all he had to do was spread his cheeks every now and then. Well, lady, shit! No man could go years in that piss-hole without a woman. And everybody did it, even the Jews, even those fucking sanctimonious Jehovah's Witnesses. And, Christ, those Gypsy guys always had it up one another. Hot people. It happens everywhere. You're healthy and you need it.

"The other prisoners hated the SS's bum boys. The prisoners hated all the faggots, but they hated the bum boys worse. I was able to do a lot for Dieter, make life a lot fucking easier for him. I got him office duty and he was smart. He could do anything. Good organizer. And he knew how to keep his mouth shut and keep out of trouble. You had to like him. I grew fond of him, even helped him make a little money. He could sew. I'm one of the best machinists going, but you had to give it to him: he had clever hands, could do anything with that sewing machine I scrounged up for him. I told the officers he could do alterations and he did all their work. Even made fat old Baumer look good in his uniform. Saved them wasting time at a tailor's when they were on leave. Then one of the wives asked him to make her a gown because she couldn't get to Berlin to shop before some big party. He got a good business going. He could buy himself all kinds of things. But he never got above himself. Smart boy.

"It was hard not to like him. You grow fond of what you fuck. It happens. He was good as a wife. Better. No shit from him like that cunt I married. Well, everything was a little crazy and he was a good boy."

Kleber looked as if he were about to weep. He took a long drink and blew his nose. Sybella said to Kleber, "It's so close in here. Could you please open a window?"

Kleber stared around anxiously, as if he had forgotten he had windows and where they were. But he said with a nastily mock graciousness, "Anything for the lovely lady," and went to the window. It was marbled with dirt and he opened it a few inches. The hard light that came in sharpened the edges of the room and Sybella's attention was drawn to something near the window. She couldn't believe what she was certain she saw.

But she forced her attention back to Kleber, who was lighting the butt-end of a cigar.

"Where was I? Oh shit, yes. The little faggot did me in the eye. I'd know better now and he didn't get everything, but goddamned near. He left me just enough to save my ass, but not much more. He took most of it. A fortune."

Sybella translated for Paul and punctuated with a shrug, having no idea what Kleber was talking about. Kleber understood.

"I'm talking about the gold, about a fucking fortune. If a man wasn't a fool, he looked after himself in Flossenbürg. We all did. There was lots for everyone. More than enough. And I don't mean the cheap shit like the clothes and books and all that crap the prisoners brought on the trains."

Kleber could see that Sybella still didn't understand. He smiled at her and it made her shift uncomfortably. She hated that he was so nastily amused by her. He looked at her smart dress, her sheer stockings and good shoes, and decided to have fun with the lady, with this fine fucking grand lady who looked as if butter wouldn't melt in her mouth. He'd make her understand.

"I'm talking about what we took off the stiffs. We took what they carried when they arrived, but we knew they hid the good stuff and they could be clever shits. They might be scared, but they weren't too scared to be goddamned clever. But there's just so many places you can hide things on a body. You ever thought about that, ma'am?

"And Flossenbürg wasn't the worst camp. There were lots worse, but most of those idiots didn't know they'd hit it lucky. But they knew they were in some shit when they saw the place. Just wasn't as deep there.

"The train would pull in and they'd just throw themselves off to get air. Usually closed in on those trains for days. No toilets. We all hated reception duty. Christ, the smell when they opened those train doors and the stink of that lot. They'd get off the trains looking like rabbits. Noses going sniff-sniff, twitch-twitch. But the pickings were nothing on reception duty.

"They combed the good stuff into their hair, sewed it into their clothes, shoved it up their asses and in their cunts. We usually had to wait till they were dead, but we finally got it. We learned to wait. No hurry. Where were they going?

"Sorting out the dead bodies was shitty duty, but we all wanted it. There were dozens of corpses every day and they could be good pickings. But you had to work fast and be pretty clever. The gold teeth were the hardest to get. Had to hammer them out and you'd be all sweaty from doing it and it took time. The stuff they sewed in their clothes was easiest to get. We all knew that, and there'd be fights over it. You got quick at cutting the stuff out of their clothes with razors. Of course we weren't supposed to keep what we found. Our orders were to turn it over to the officers, who'd send it to the Fatherland for the war effort. Big laugh. Big bullshit! You know how much would get to the Fatherland. Just enough to make them think we were doing our job. The officers kept most of it. We were even searched after we harvested the stiffs. And that's where Dieter came in handy. He sewed secret pockets into my clothes and he was clever. He put hiding places in collars and cuffs where the cloth was thick and a quick frisk wouldn't get it. No matter what I wanted to hide, it didn't leave a bulge. The other poor buggers had to shove the really valuable stuff up their asses if they wanted to hold on to it. I wish I still had that jacket he made me. It's a collector's item. All that old shit from the war brings good prices these days. And that jacket has a real history."

Kleber was warming to his story, because he could see its awful effect on Sybella and Paul. Well, if they didn't want to hear it, they could ask him to stop.

"I wasn't greedy. I even gave Dieter some gold. I'd put a little piece up his ass and screw him. It turned me on. He was a good lay, but not worth all that gold. But then, there was plenty and always more to come. Besides, we were winning the war.

"I even got to use my trade. I'm a machinist, so I turned my gold into wire. Easy to hide, easy to get out. I had to be very clever to get it done, but I'm no fool and I did it. Yards and yards of gold wire. I electroplated it with copper and wound the armature of a motor with it. There was a pump that didn't work and it had a big motor, and it just sat with all the other junk over behind the kitchen building. I took the copper off the armature and every chance I got I wound the gold wire around it. This old beat-up pump that nobody ever looked at was worth a fortune.

"Near the end they shipped more and more undesirables to us at Flossenbürg. Hundreds more than we could handle. Christ, what a mess. It was always more people and less food. That's crazy. Those fucking people in Berlin just sent out orders. They didn't have to think about how we were going to carry them out. With less food these new ones couldn't work, they died faster, but what the hell could we do? And we were sending some of them out to work in an aircraft factory and we had to keep that lot working for the war, so they had to get a little more food. I don't know how we did it, but we kept that factory going. Problems all the time, nothing but problems. And it all fell on us. Berlin didn't care who died, but they wanted to get work out of them. Even we couldn't get work out of the dead. It's stupid to train somebody to do a job and then let them starve to death. It doesn't make any fucking sense. No wonder we lost. It still makes me mad to think about it."

Kleber's voice had grown more and more excited as he relived his frustration. He scrubbed at his forehead as if to erase the troubling memories. He closed his eyes and drained his glass, fell back as if exhausted by the effort of that long-ago work. He snapped to alertness when he saw Sybella heading toward the window and shouted angrily, "Where are you going?"

"I'm going to open the window more."

"Get away from there. I'll do it." He waited till she was back in her chair before he went sullenly to the window and opened it fractionally wider. But she'd gotten close enough to be sure. It made terrible sense.

"It gets cold in here. It's always fucking cold in here. There's never any heat. It's always cold."

Paul looked at Sybella with concern and reached across to take her hand, asking, "Are you all right? You don't look well."

"I'll get through. He can't take much longer."

Kleber said something and Sybella translated, "He said you should have some schnapps."

"Tell him to just get to the point," Paul said, not looking at Kleber.

Sybella repeated Paul's instruction, courteously reworded, and Kleber shrugged and spoke: "Not much left to tell. It all turned to shit, but you know that. It was spring. Can't ever forget it. April. You were coming, Mister American. We could even hear the bombing from the camp. You were in my country killing my people, taking over. Well, that was a long time ago. Let bygones be bygones, I always say. Thirty years, but I can still see it.

"Dieter kept saying they were coming and I should get away quickly. Silly little shit. I knew that. But where would I run? Now I know why he was anxious to get me on my way. He wanted to get to the gold. He had plans."

Sybella could only translate the words, not his mincing imitation of Dieter as he piped, "'You must save yourself, Kleber. You must run. They won't harm me, but they can do terrible things to you. They might even kill you, my one, my only, my true love. I'll bring the gold and we'll buy new lives and go away and be together.' I believed his fucking fairy story, so I got ready. He found me civilian clothes to wear. Good clothes. Too fucking good. Looked like a banker.

"What could I do? There wasn't time. I got as much of the gold as I could off of the motor and wound it around my ankles under my socks and around my waist. And I got my ass out of there. A close thing. I'm running up this road and I can see the dust in the air from the American trucks coming along behind me. Then some fucking SS bigwig races by me all alone in the back of his limousine and I'm hauling my ass up the road wondering how the fuck I'm going to outrun the American army.

"Most of us had forged papers we'd had made, just in case. Mine were for a machinist who had a heart problem that kept him out of the army. I'm supposed to be a worker and there I am running up the road from the camp dressed liked a god-damned banker.

"It took me two months to get to my sister's, which is where I told Dieter he could find me. Hah!

"The gold I had didn't last long. My sister had five kids and no husband and no food. The black market took it all, just so we could eat. Christ knows where my wife had got to, and who cared? And that little shit Dieter was somewhere with my gold.

"Took years, but I finally found him. A fucking lot of good it did me."

Kleber fell silent, deep in his festering grief. For a moment he looked as if he had fallen asleep and then his head popped up.

"He owed me," he said furiously. "My sister was dying of cancer in 1965. I had to take her to Munich to a specialist and Christ knows we couldn't even pay the doctor she had at home, much less a big-city one. But I did my best. Blood is blood. We were in Munich walking to the doctor's and then I see him; there's Dieter's picture in this store window, one of those expensive places near the opera. It was his face, but not his name. His picture, but he wasn't Dieter Holtman anymore. He was Helmut Kiel now. He was this famous dress designer.

"I wanted to find him and kill him. I can't afford to save my sister's life and he's rich, with his own factory and everybody knows about him. And he did it with my money. I called his office for weeks and I could never get past his fucking secretary. And what could I do? He knew I couldn't show myself. I'd been a patriot, did as my country wanted, and that made me a criminal now. I got shit for being a soldier. No pensions, no great hospitals to go to like you Americans. I was a criminal and all that thieving faggot had to do was get his hands on me and turn me over to the authorities. No wonder I wanted to kill him. I've had years to think about how I'd do it, and I'd make it very special."

Paul asked Sybella, "Do you know this Kiel he's talking about?"

"He's very famous, Paul. Won't be hard to find."

"Still, ask Kleber if he has his address."

She asked and Kleber said, "Yes, but money first."

Paul said wearily to Sybella, "Give him the money."

Sybella saw the greedy look spring to Kleber's face and it confirmed her guess that he understood English. She opened her purse and took out the thick envelope. She put it into Kleber's anxiously extended hands and said in English, "You'll want to count it."

He counted the money and then counted it again, as Sybella and Paul sat, their attention fixed on Kleber's avaricious face.

Kleber stood holding the money in both hands against his chest, then rushed away and behind the curtain that led to the other room, careening drunkenly in his haste, and they heard the clatter of what sounded like pots and pans being thrown about.

Kleber came back into the room unsteadily, now showing fully the effects of the bottle of schnapps he had almost finished. He handed a slip of paper to Sybella, who read the address, nodded to Paul, and said, "It seems right."

Kleber glared at Paul and said in passable English, "You could have afforded more. What I said was worth more. I should have asked for more. You're related. I can see it. And he said he didn't have any family. You'll find him and get money out of him. And you'll tell him about this shitty old drunk you gave all your precious money to. I saw you looking at me as if I was shit. I'm not a monster. I've read all that crap about how we are bad people. We shouldn't have done this and that. We should have resisted those awful Nazis. Who can do that? Who does that? Who says no to the big guys? Your country tells you to kill and you goddamned well kill. We lost. That's what we did wrong."

Paul rose and helped Sybella up, saying, "Let's get out of here."

Kleber stumbled after them, whining, "You could have afforded more. But I don't even need your fucking money. Ask that fairy if he's still got my gold up his ass. He'll know what I mean."

Paul moved toward the door, leading Sybella, but with a speed that astonished them, Kleber pushed in front of Paul, and Paul tensed and shoved Kleber out of their way. Kleber fell against the wall, keening, "So much like him."

Paul fumbled the locks open, tugged the door ajar, and tried to pull Sybella past Kleber, but Kleber clung to his sleeve, weeping, and slurring, "You could have afforded more. You could! You could! You're shit!"

Paul asked, "What the hell's he saying?"

Sybella answered, "That he's a greedy fool."

They were out the door and scuttling down the stairs as Kleber screamed after, "You're shit. Shit! Shit!" Even as they hurried down the alley, they could still hear him howling.

⸘

At the airport, Paul booked them on the first flight out of Berlin. In the ladies' room, Sybella copied the address from Kleber's soiled scrap, burned the dirty paper, and washed her hands. Then she washed them again.

A little over two hours later they were back in their Munich flat. She ran a bath and planned to soak for the rest of the day. Paul went across the street to buy pastry and came back to find her in the bath and finally looking calm. He brought the box into the bathroom and opened it for her inspection. He'd bought her favorite éclairs.

Sybella finally emerged, wearing her floor-length red terry robe, shiny with steam, her hair in damp strands around her face.

Paul heard her in the kitchen and followed her movements in his mind's eye, his pen poised above his notebook.

She came to stand over him, holding the last bite of an éclair in front of him which he snapped from her fingers. She licked her fingers, then put her hands on his shoulders, asking, "What are you writing?"

How should he phrase his answer? Finally, "It's a letter to him, to my father. If I don't do it right away I may never be able to."

He put down his pen and pulled her onto his lap.

"Careful," she said, "I'm sticky. Aren't you hungry?"

"A while ago I thought I'd never want to eat again. Jesus, what an ugly experience." He squeezed her. "Thank God you were with me. I can't imagine getting through that alone."

"I'm glad you didn't have to."

–174–

She started to rise, but he pulled her back. She said, "I'm going to run you a bath," and he said, "Wait. I want you to hear the start of this. I'd like to finish it and get it right into the mail, before I have a chance to think too much. And then I'm going to take us for the best dinner Munich has to offer."

Sybella leaned back against him and the scent of soap that rose from her smelled of domesticity and safety, and it was consoling to find sanity in something as simple as soap and cleanliness. He had been too near the filthy machinery of death that day. He picked up his much-edited sheet of paper and read, "Dear Mr. Kiel: I've located you through a mutual acquaintance. I learned from my mother, Leda Kohl, that you were her close friend when she lived in Berlin in 1935. As you may know, my mother died some months ago. During her last days she spoke of you often and fondly. I'm in Munich for an indefinite stay and would welcome the chance to meet you, as my mother remained concerned about your well-being. It was her last wish that I try and find you. I would like to carry out her wish."

"You don't want to tell him what you know?" Sybella asked neutrally.

"I don't know how to and I don't want to force a meeting. I have to face the fact that it might be best if we never meet. It might be painful for both of us. It's over forty years and he's been through things I only had to listen to today, and I'm still shaken."

Sybella considered and nodded. "Then it's a good letter."

"I've been writing and thinking that maybe what I was meant to get from all this was meeting you. Perhaps I should leave the past alone. I feel happier and more peaceful than I ever imagined I could. Even the five thousand to that monster is a bargain."

Sybella considered and nodded. Then she asked, "Do you think I'm sane? By and large, I mean."

Paul made a show of giving the matter serious consideration before saying, "Well..."

"Thanks," she said, tapping him on the forehead with her knuckle. "I'm serious. I doubted my sanity at Kleber's. Up near the window, you remember? I went to open it wider and he got furious. It wasn't air I wanted; I wanted a closer look at a picture sitting on a chair. I studied art history and if I'm not mad, Paul, I think Kleber has a picture by Brueghel the Elder sitting in the middle of that squalor. It has to be worth a fortune. It's probably catalogued with the loot the Nazis made off with. Can he possibly be living like that and not know that picture is worth a fortune?"

Paul considered, then smiled nastily and said, "I sincerely hope so."

{

A week after they mailed the letter to Kiel, a man took up an observation post at the pastry shop's sidewalk cafe across from their building. He was there, on and off, for only two days, not long enough to become obvious or interesting to the cafe's owner, but long enough to find out what he had come to learn. He didn't even follow Sybella and Paul every time they went out and only risked photographing them once with a tiny Minox. The picture turned out clearly and his client wrote him a check when he delivered the print. The client even complimented the man: "Fine work. As competent as always. Let's hope this pair is the last."

Chapter 6

The caller's precise German-accented English and overly courteous manner tinged what he said with menace.

"I am an associate of Mr. Kiel," the caller began. "It is about your letter to him. It is a matter of some concern to him. Do I express that properly? He is in receipt of your letter, but puzzled by what it is you wish from him."

"I don't wish anything from Mr. Kiel," Paul answered, feeling irritated at being questioned by a stranger about his very personal letter and his intentions.

"Perhaps you could tell me more about what it is you want to discuss with Mr. Kiel."

"I can't. More to the point, I don't want to. If Mr. Kiel doesn't want to see me, just say so."

"Perhaps I'm giving the wrong impression. Mr. Kiel is a very busy man and I screen such personal requests."

"Has he seen my letter?"

"Most certainly, Mr. Howe."

"Does he remember my mother? Perhaps I was mistaken about who he is."

The man evaded the question by saying, "Mr. Kiel did live in Berlin at that time."

"That's not what I asked."

"Let me say that letters like yours have presented problems in the past. I would like to ... to determine the nature of your interest. That is all."

"Then tell me if Mr. Kiel knew my mother. I may have been misled about who he is. If that's so, this conversation is pointless."

Paul was sure that the man covered the receiver and spoke to someone. Was Kiel there? Was Kiel directing this conversation? What the hell was going on?

After a long pause the man said, "Mr. Kiel knew a woman much like Leda Kohl in 1935."

"Oh, for Christ's sake. Did he or didn't he?"

"I'm unable to say more at this time."

"And when the hell will you be able to say more?"

"I would think a meeting would be helpful. I do not wish to make you angry, but there are good reasons which I am sure you would understand, if I might explain in person."

Making no effort to keep the sharpness out of his voice, Paul said, "If Mr. Kiel feels it necessary to screen me, I suppose I have no choice. What does Mr. Kiel think I'm up to?"

"He can't be sure, you see. As I said, there have been problems in the past. He has become cautious. He does not mean to give offense, nor do I. I was going to suggest we meet near your apartment in the Englisher Garten tomorrow at three in the afternoon, if that's agreeable."

"You could come here."

"I would prefer we meet alone. The woman..."

"How do you know there's a woman with me?"

The caller ignored the question and asked, "Is my suggestion agreeable?"

"Why the hell all this mystery?"

"If you would prefer not..."

"All right. In the English Gardens. Where?"

"In front of the Chinesischer Turm."

"What's that?"

"The Tower. The Chinese Tower. Tomorrow at three. I'll know you, Mr. Howe."

"How?" Paul asked, but the man had hung up. Paul put the receiver down and was surprised to see that his hand shook.

The hundreds of mystery novels Paul had read had not prepared him for murky secretiveness in his own life, and he felt uneasy and threatened. It took several minutes for him to realize something that should have made him wary from the start: how had the caller gotten his phone number? It was listed under the apartment owner's name. He hadn't included the number in his note, just his address. Someone had gone to some trouble to discover it. But how? From the address alone? And they had found out more; they knew about Sybella. He had an intense need to tell her about the call. Where had she said she was going shopping?

He needed air. He decided on the cafe across the way, from where he could see his doorway and watch for Sybella. He grabbed the doorknob and stopped. Whoever the caller was, he knew things about Paul not mentioned in the letter, while Paul knew nothing about the wary caller or Kiel. Had they been watching him? Would someone be watching when he left his building? He opened the door a crack and examined the people outside, looking for anyone who showed interest in his building. He was surprised at how frightened he felt. Mysteries were entertaining on the page, but deeply disturbing in the real world.

He felt simultaneously afraid, idiotic, and exposed as he walked nervously to the cafe.

As he sat considering a third pastry, he saw Sybella struggling up the street, laden with shopping bags. He hurried to her and she was surprised to see him. He took a couple of bags from her and led her to his table as she protested mildly, "I should get some of these things into the refrigerator. I bought fish. Something's the matter. You look upset."

"Have something to eat. I want to stay here awhile." He signaled for the waitress and glanced around. Just strollers and shoppers but, by now, everybody looked suspect. Well, let them spy on him. He hadn't done anything. Yet he felt he had. He explained the call to Sybella, seasoning his account with an anger underneath which she sensed his fear. His fear was catching and, as usual, her fear went to her stomach and it rolled over, making her smile wryly, because her worst moments always voiced themselves in comic noises.

"I resent the way he contacted me," Paul said. "Using some assistant to check me out. It was insulting. And we've been spied on. He knows about you. He's invaded our privacy and he has no right. I've half a mind not to meet him. Let him go screw."

"Can you stop now, let this whole thing go?" Sybella asked.

"No, of course I can't. I have to meet the sonuvabitch."

§

The day of the meeting, Paul hid his feelings in silence and unaccustomed behavior: he lingered in the bath, shaved with immaculate care, and took pains choosing what he would wear, despite the fact that rain slammed against the windows in sheets. He didn't have to tell Sybella how he was feeling; she could see it in his stiff movements and in the way he picked at his lunch.

At two o'clock, Paul pulled a chair near the window and sat staring through the rain at some distant anxiety. At five minutes to three he rose weightily, heaving out of the chair with an old man's sigh. "I'd better be going."

"Take my umbrella. You'll get soaked."

"It's only a few minutes away. I've got my raincoat."

"You'll still get soaked."

"It's purple."

"What?"

"Your umbrella's purple. It's a lady's umbrella."

"So what?"

"Men don't carry that kind of umbrella. I'd look silly."

"You'd look dry."

"I don't want the damned umbrella."

"Then get wet."

By way of apology, he touched her arm. "Being dry isn't going to do a damned thing to improve my rotten mood. I feel like someone in a Jack Higgins thriller. I'm even wearing one of those spy raincoats. If I'm not back by sundown, call out the posse."

He gave her a kiss in passing, then went back and gave her a long one, and hurried off before his small measure of courage ran out.

He crossed Leopoldstrasse into the park, already soaked and irritated with himself for fussing about the umbrella and then not taking it. By the time he was in the English Garden and had found the path to the Tower, he was feeling as foul as the weather. He chewed on his grievance at being put through an interview, and raged at Kiel and at the man he was going to meet. He reached the Chinese Tower that mimicked the one in London's Kew Garden, but saw no one waiting, which intensified his anger. He himself was late, and that man still wasn't there. As he circled the tower he saw a man emerge from beneath a tree near the path.

Paul watched him approach, feeling combative, his stance and expression radiating belligerence, hardly noticing the rain that was running down his face and underneath his collar. He could barely see the approaching man for his immense black umbrella and the soft hat he wore low on his forehead.

When the man was several feet away he stopped and called, "There's a cafe down this way. We can be dry there."

"This should be quick," Paul called back. "We can talk here."

The man shrugged and came to Paul. Both edged close to the tower, though it offered no shelter. The man moved his umbrella over Paul, but Paul stepped out from under its protection. When Paul could bring himself to look, he saw a young man — late twenties? — certainly younger than he was. The man looked mild and not at all threatening.

"I don't like the idea of this meeting," Paul said. "I only want to meet Mr. Kiel and I resent being screened as if I was applying for a job. And how the hell did you get my phone number? How did you know about Miss Walter?"

"I'm sorry, Mr. Howe, but I already have a cold and I'm afraid it will get worse if we stand here long. May we please get to someplace dry?"

"Oh!" Paul said, disappointed at having his anger diluted by reasonableness. "Yes, sure."

The man took a step, then turned and said, "I have no manners. My name is Conrad Dietz." Paul took the offered hand, shook it briefly, and they headed down the path Dietz indicated, Paul maintaining his distance by still refusing to share Dietz's umbrella.

The cafe lay just around the first turn in the path and was almost empty, except for a couple who sat in a far corner, deep in an obviously distressing conversation. A heavyset woman stood behind the counter, but didn't look up from her book when they came in. The cold fluorescent light made the room seem chillier than it was. Dietz went to the corner table farthest from the counter and the agitated couple, and Paul followed. Dietz removed his hat and held it away from himself with distaste, looking around for someplace to put the offendingly wet thing, finally hooking it over the back of the chair next to him. Playing the host, Dietz gestured Paul to a chair and asked what he would like.

"Just coffee, thank you," Paul said, struggling out of his wet coat.

"Cream?"

"Black."

Paul watched Dietz at the counter and listened without understanding as he chatted with the waitress, apparently saying something funny, because she laughed.

Dietz was a tall blond with a receding hairline. Paul now saw he must be thirty-five or so, slim, with a round open face and large, china blue eyes. But Paul thought he might be younger than his guess, because of Dietz's manner, the way he moved, his aura of shy uncertainty.

Dietz returned with the coffees in Styrofoam cups and two pale pastries in clear plastic packages. He said, "I thought you might like something to eat."

Paul wrapped his hands around his cup in a vain effort to drive the damp out, and, trying to reclaim the upper hand, said, "Now, what the hell is this all about?"

"I really don't like to persist or irritate, but can you tell me why you would like to see Mr. Kiel?"

"I want to know why you don't want me to see him. He could have ignored my letter. Instead, I've apparently been investigated, and I'm meeting you like somebody in a spy movie."

Dietz regarded Paul appraisingly. Paul looked open and direct, but all Americans looked that way to Dietz, even that terrible fraud, Mr. Atkins, who had almost cost Mr. Kiel so much money a few years before.

Dietz said, "The problem is that your mother didn't know Mr. Kiel. She did know a Dieter Holtman in 1935. And that's the difficulty. No one from that time knows a Mr. Kiel, because there was no such person. That's been a problem for us. For Mr. Kiel, I mean. There have been several people from that time who have tried to take financial advantage of their knowledge. You're the first in five years to approach us. We thought all that was finally over. The law has been changed, you know. Even with the old law, the efforts of those others never worked. They got nothing. However, Mr. Kiel has learned a caution. We looked into you, only because it is prudent to know something of those who write these letters. We use a firm to check such people out. We discovered Leda Kohl did indeed have a son. You may be he, but, even if you are, you may be a black sheep."

"If you were afraid of blackmail, you could have saved your money. It cost me five thousand dollars to locate Mr. Kiel, to say nothing of what it has cost me to come and stay here while I looked for him."

"You say you paid someone to lead you to Mr. Kiel?" Dietz asked, his expression clearly declaring that his guard had gone up.

"When my mother knew she was dying she started talking about her life in Germany before the war. She'd never spoken of it before. Too awful, and too many regrets. She talked a lot about a man named Rudy Mueller who disappeared and about Dieter Holtman, the man she was living with when he was arrested."

"That doesn't answer why meeting Mr. Kiel is worth five thousand dollars."

Paul didn't know how to answer, without saying more than he felt able to. He evaded, "I put ads in German papers asking for information that would help me find Dieter Holtman. A man named Horst Kleber finally answered."

Dietz's expression of distaste showed Paul that Dietz knew of Kleber. "You met him?" Dietz asked.

"In East Berlin. A terrible man in a terrible place. He wanted five thousand for what he knew. He talked about knowing Holtman in the Flossenbürg camp and that he had found him years later, but that Holtman now called himself Helmut Kiel."

"Excuse my pressing, Mr. Howe, but why so much effort and money? You must help me to understand."

"When Holtman was arrested, my mother ran, made it out of Germany that same day. Lawyers and bribery couldn't find Holtman. But she felt responsible, right to the end. In fact, there's half a million dollars set aside by her estate for him. She thought he might need it."

Paul could see from Dietz's expression that this implied bribe had worked no better than his other evasions, that for all the mildness Paul saw, Dietz was perceptive and tenacious. Paul said, "There is more to it than that, but I just can't tell anyone but Kiel what that is. It's personal. It has to do with my mother."

For the first time, Dietz sensed Paul's difficulty and that, whatever the man's purpose, it was not just another attempt at extortion. Dietz said, "You must understand that you found Mr. Kiel through a man who tried blackmail several times, said he would make damaging revelations, would tell the world that this famous designer is a homosexual, wore the pink triangle in the camps. When he wasn't threatening, he wrote these awful begging letters ... two and three a week. They were almost worse than the threats. He has the crazy idea that Mr. Kiel should help him for old times' sake. The man must be mad. But there have been many like him over the years. None of these people ever got a cent.

"For a while there was some danger to Mr. Kiel, because many homosexuals were sent back to jail when they were found after the war, despite having been in the camps. That's not done now. However, it would still be disagreeable for Mr. Kiel to have all that raked up. As I said, it's been five years since the last person showed up wanting money. Now you come and say you don't want money, that you paid to find him. You must understand that I can only wonder why. Mr. Kiel also wonders why. And what can I tell him? If you really want to see him, you will have to tell me why."

They'd come full circle. Paul wondered why he himself hadn't foreseen that his pursuit would lead to one very basic question he should have asked himself: What do you want from Kiel? Self-knowledge? An end to a story? A father? What?

Paul blustered, "I don't have to explain myself to you. And who the hell are you to ask these questions? What's your connection to Kiel? Is this part of your job?"

"No, Mr. Howe, I'm his lover."

"And I'm his son."

Dietz stiffened. "Prove it," he snapped, but when the veil of surprise lifted, he looked closely at Paul and knew the truth, almost laughed at the unlikely, but now obvious, fact.

Paul was as stunned by the absolute sureness in his own words as he was astonished by what Dietz had said. He had gotten used to the idea of an aging homosexual as his father, a father who had experienced the degradation of a concentration camp, a frail old father, a victim in a shawl. Instead, he had found a man of substance who had a young lover. His father had come suddenly and vividly alive, and Paul saw how absurd the script he'd written for himself and Kiel was.

Dietz's mind raced over the possibilities of what Paul had said, but he couldn't organize his thoughts, could only say lamely, "Mr. Kiel doesn't know. I'm sure he doesn't. But you do have something of his look, as he must have been."

"Oh, stop calling him Mr. Kiel. What goes on between you two must be a lot less formal."

"I'm thirty-three and I have called him Mr. Kiel since I went to work for him fifteen years ago, and that is what I've called him even after we became lovers. You fall out of the sky and you are belligerent, and you tell me extraordinary things that may or may not be true.

"If you are insistent," Dietz continued tensely, "you will find a way to reach Mr. Kiel and tell him your story, true or not. I won't be able to stop you, although I'll certainly try. But there are things you should know before you do. Mr. Kiel's health is poor. He finds it more and more difficult to carry on a large business. We are close to completing arrangements for his retirement. Your appearance, your 'news' ... so sudden, so unexpected ... would be a shock I would sooner spare him. You may not want money, but you want something from him, something for yourself, and I am not sure you have the right to ask for anything. It is plain that you do not like the idea of my being his lover, but I do love him. I have for many years and I've been good for him, as he has for me. And what will you give him? A son? And just what is he supposed to do about you? What worries me is what you want and what you'll take."

"I don't want anything. You needn't worry that he'll leave any of his money to me."

"You have a very ugly streak, Mr. Howe. I don't like the idea of your meeting him, stirring up that awful time. It has taken years for him to get past what happened, to stop worrying that he might have to serve out the ten years remaining on his sentence. Only in the last few years has he slept without nightmares. Now you want to bring all that back in a way that could be very awful. I ask you to think about that."

"And what, in Christ's name, is so terrible about his knowing he has a son?"

"He may not want a son. Do you want a man you've never met as your father? You have more power to hurt Mr. Kiel than any of the blackmailers." Paul felt foolish at not having thought through to the consequences of what he had set out to do.

"We seem caught, Mr. Howe. You've come a long way to find Mr. Kiel. If you are his son, I have no right to keep you from him. I'd fail if I tried. But I want to protect him from being hurt."

"You mean protect him from me."

"If you can hurt him, yes. It is painful to see someone you love get hurt. I love him a great deal, because I know him. I don't know you. And, despite any blood relationship, you don't know him or what he's been through. We have a dilemma. I should say, *I* have a dilemma. But you can help, if you would, and it might be best all around. That is, it might be best for you, too."

"You don't have to suggest anything," Paul said. "There's no point, because whatever it is, you're probably right."

"About what?"

"Everything. I'll stay away, leave things as they are. You can tell him I was just another person looking for money. My mother's will says that if I can't find him, the money goes to charity. He doesn't need it, and the chance that he might is what worried her. I'll have done all I could."

"I must be perverse. You say you'll go away, but I don't like the idea that I'm driving you away. In the long run that may not be the best thing. Perhaps there's a compromise."

"I don't want a compromise. I should say, I don't need one."

"At least hear it."

Paul listened to Dietz, but couldn't agree to anything, because he could barely think. How could he decide? What Dietz was suggesting felt impossible to him, emotional miles beyond his abilities. He had to think. He had to get away from here, away from this man. He asked for time to think.

"How long will you need?" Dietz asked.

Paul wasn't sure, but he said, "Not long."

"When?"

"Not long."

"Would a couple of hours be enough?"

"Don't press me."

"Are you feeling all right?"

"No."

"I'll stay in town for a while at our flat here and get into some dry clothes. Here's my card, you can call me there."

Paul took the card. He asked Dietz, "If I don't call, what will you tell him?"

"What you suggested. That you were not who your note said, that you'd never met Leda Kohl, just heard of her through Kleber; that you were part of another of Kleber's schemes."

The idea of that explanation hurt, but it would serve.

Dietz looked at Paul with concern: the man looked ill. Dietz said, "I'll walk you to your door."

"You needn't."

"I know. Come along."

They moved from the sheltering doorway and up the street, not hurrying, both huddled under the umbrella, Paul too drenched and weary to care about the teeming rain. At his door, Paul turned to Dietz and said, "There may be another problem. You think I look something like Mr. Kiel. If we meet, do you think he'll see that?"

"One of the awful things that's happening to Mr. Kiel is that he is having vision problems. And so much of his pleasure in life has always come from what he saw. This time, sad to say, it may spare us all difficulty."

⸙

Sybella struggled to get Paul out of the sopping clothes that clung to him. He seemed spent, unable to help himself. She wrapped him in her own vast robe and sat him in the kitchen where the oven was warm from the dinner she was preparing. Then she filled the tub and helped him in.

Sybella brought her cup of tea into the bathroom, sat on the low metal drying stool, and watched Paul. She sensed she shouldn't speak, although she churned with questions: What happened? Will you meet Mr. Kiel? What was the man like?

She tried to look calm and sat gazing around the all-white room which seemed too intensely white, like being in an overexposed picture where even the vivid red of her dress looked faded.

Only Paul's head rose above the water as he lay still, staring over the edge of the vast tub, trying not to relive his encounter with Dietz and unable to do anything else. Failing forgetfulness, he tried to fathom the tumultuous reactions that made him feel so spent.

He finally said, "The man I met – this Dietz – is my father's lover."

Sybella said, "Ah," as neutrally as she could.

"My father has a young lover and the idea makes me nuts. I hate him for having one. I'm a red-blooded American man and we don't ever touch one another. I've just proved how all-American I am and made a fool of myself. I couldn't even get close enough to Dietz to share his umbrella. I showed him; I got soaked. Life can be the damnedest farce. What the hell am I doing here?"

She'd hoped she was part of his reason, but didn't say so. Instead, she asked, "Will you go home?" in a voice more calm than she felt.

"Would it matter?"

"Very much," she answered. "Yes, very much indeed, Paul. I probably shouldn't admit it, but I'd manage. I always seem to manage. I sometimes wish I were one of those women who fall apart, but I'm not."

"When I started feeling I was in over my head with Dietz, all I wanted to do was run back here, run home. Dietz asked why I wanted to see Kiel and I had a hard time answering, so I came up with some reasons that didn't ring true, even to myself. Isn't everyone supposed to want to know who his father is? But what then? What if you don't like him, or he doesn't like you?"

He said, "May I have a sip of your tea?"

He put his hand over hers as she held her cup to his lips, then took her hand and kissed it. She pressed her hand to his lips, then went back to her seat.

"Dietz offered me a compromise, and I don't want a compromise. You see, while I may not know what I want, I want *all* of whatever it is, even if it's nothing. No compromise. I seem to be out to prove that I can be as stupid as the next guy."

"What does Dietz suggest?"

"That I go to their home and meet my father, but not tell him that he's my father unless I feel I must, unless I feel that it's truly for the best."

Paul looked at Sybella for her reaction, but couldn't see her expression, for she was looking down into her cup. He waited until she looked up and asked, "Well?"

"It gives you time to think, to meet him and make your decision about a real person. You've been chasing some character in your mother's story. Isn't just meeting him and telling him what happened to your mother part of what you want, what you promised?"

"I think I could go if you came with me."

"Of course," she said, and went to kiss him on top of his head. "I must check on dinner." At the door she stopped and looked around the room. "Why does this room seem so *white* white? It's blinding."

"We'll paint it."

"Your lease is only for two more months."

"We'll paint it anyway. May as well have what we like, while we look for something bigger."

Chapter 7

Two days later, Paul and Sybella drove the route Dietz had drawn on a map and sent by messenger. They headed toward Tegernsee and the exclusive monied enclaves that lay near Munich. Dietz had offered to send a car and driver, but Paul declined, preferring to be alone with Sybella on the trip, and, if he couldn't go on, to be able to turn back without explanation.

As they neared their destination, the houses grew gradually grander, the acreage of each vaster, and the landscaping more elaborate. Soon, in the ultimate accession to the status of mansion, no houses could be seen from the road, for they lay deep within vast grounds. They passed rock walls broken only by elaborate wrought-iron gates that opened onto tree-lined drives.

"There!" Sybella shouted, then screeched to a stop and backed up. She turned off the road and drove up to an immense gate of intricate iron flora with gilt details. Paul got out and went to the intercom embedded in the gate's stone support. He announced himself and, with a barely audible click, the massive gates fell silently back. He returned to the car and they drove through, moving up a winding road flanked by venerable firs.

Paul remarked, "I feel as if I'm going to Oz. Will the Wizard be a kind man? Does he grant wishes?

"Please, stay near me," he said. "And if I start making a damned fool of myself, get me out of there."

"I think that if you made a fool of yourself, I'd understand. Good Lord, how far is this place? We seem to be halfway back to Munich." They rounded a sharp bend. "Ah, there it is. Very impressive."

It was like so many large homes he had stayed in from Newport to Bombay with his mother, as much declarations of status as of difference. He wondered who had built this replica of an English Tudor manor house in the middle of Germany.

Before they came to a stop at the entrance, a butler was already coming toward the car. He opened Sybella's door and bowed her out. She was impressed. It seemed so well rehearsed.

"If you would please follow me," the butler said in German and led them through a broad, beautiful rose-and-gold central hall that ran the considerable depth of the house to a terrace set high above a man-made lake and elaborately groomed formal gardens.

Restrained politeness gave a wary air to the introductions. Dietz presented Sybella to Mr. Kiel, who stood with difficulty and took her hand. He then introduced Paul to Mr. Kiel. Paul took his father's hand and felt its warm soft reality, amazed at how eerily simple it was to reach across years of anonymity and find a phantom turned suddenly mortal. Was it really this easy to face one's unknown father after so long? Paul barely managed to articulate a polite greeting through the breaking wave of emotion that deafened him to the sound of his own voice. He could only tell he had spoken by the acknowledging smile on Kiel's face. Kiel said with warmth, "How very nice to meet you, Mr. Howe. Please, sit down."

They took their places at a table elegantly set for lunch. It was bright at the unshaded table and Sybella put her sunglasses on. The butler approached deferentially as Kiel asked them what they would like to drink before lunch.

Kiel was an expert host and drew Sybella out on neutral topics: the current Klimpt show in Vienna, the opera season. They spoke English and Kiel, seeking an impersonal comment to address to Paul, said, "English is one of your country's gifts to me, Mr. Howe. I even know some slang, but it's World War II vintage. I doubt anyone still says, 'Beat me, Daddy, eight to the bar,' or, 'All reet, all root.'"

"Please call me Paul."

"Your troops arrived to recivilize my country, *Paul,*" Kiel said, testing the weight of this new man's name. "They came and stayed awhile and many of us learned English. I also learned to chew gum which is a habit I still haven't broken myself of, but that I keep private. It helps me think, or so I think."

As Kiel talked Paul took the man in and was amused at how far apart reality and expectation were. Even knowing that Kiel was a highly successful clothes designer hadn't dislodged his idea that he would find a man who wore the marks of the concentration camp — a hangdog expression, vulnerable eyes, a quivering voice, palsied hands, and a camp tattoo on his wrist. He had imagined the man in the shocking picture at Dachau, but grown old. Instead, he saw a man impeccably dressed in a beige linen suit with a dark blue shirt and striped foulard. The face was lined with a tracery of wrinkles, like crushed tissue paper, but strong bones held the skin taut. Even this near to him, Kiel looked younger than Paul knew he was. Paul wondered if this was how he would look someday and if he would ever have this man's air of complete self-containment and easy urbanity. Paul had met many like him in his mother's circle, men shiny with wealth and poise. Kiel reminded Paul vividly of his mother: she'd had the same studied ease with new people, giving off just enough warmth to draw them near enough for a closer look, but without inviting intimacy.

Paul became aware that Kiel saw the intense scrutiny he was subjecting him to. Kiel smiled, as if to tell Paul that his curiosity about Leda's old friend was understood. Kiel said he'd been rude not to ask Sybella if she would like to freshen up before lunch. She smiled her thanks, rose, and Dietz led her toward the house.

"Perhaps you would also like to freshen up before lunch?" Kiel asked Paul as they sat watching Sybella and Dietz enter the house.

"Yes, but in a minute," Paul said. "I hope you'll forgive my staring at you, but I heard so much about you from my mother that..." He couldn't quite shape coherence from the thoughts that buzzed and whirled erratically in his mind, but Kiel picked up the thread and said, "I'm touched that you tried to find me, and I apologize for our reticence, any problem we presented you. It's odd to think you found me through Kleber. Kleber, of all people. My experience of him is that he rarely does anything for nothing. I hope he wasn't too demanding."

"A little American money. Nothing excessive."

"I want very much to hear more about your mother and I've arranged for us to have some time alone after we lunch, if your young lady won't think us rude. Conrad will show Miss Walter the house while I take you through the gardens, if that's agreeable. Miss Walter seems a charming woman. I knew her former husband. I have a lot of theatre clients. I like most of them immensely and they go to the kinds of places where my clothes get shown off to good advantage."

Over lunch the conversation remained general, with Kiel leading, telling amusing stories about his customers and business, asking Paul's and Sybella's opinions on world events, suggesting esoteric sights in Munich Paul might have missed, and urging Sybella to be sure Paul saw them. He told the story of the ornate gates to the estate and how they had been saved from being melted down by the Nazis for cannon. Dietz was quiet, devoting himself to seeing that food was passed and that everyone had what they wanted. From time to time, Dietz would look at Paul and smile, although he was unable to keep concern and troubled uncertainty out of his eyes. But Kiel proved such an adept host that conversation stayed aloft and the atmosphere became pleasantly light.

As Kiel had planned, after lunch Dietz took Sybella away for a tour of the house and Kiel led Paul down the two flights of steps that led to the main garden below.

"Now," Kiel said when they reached a path bordered by rosebushes, "tell me about Leda. It hurt me a great deal to read she had died, and really so young. I know she was still beautiful, because I bought all her records, saw her in magazines. I hope the end came kindly."

Kiel bent over a rosebush and began pinching off dead blossoms, stooping to throw them under nearby bushes.

"I always wanted to see her again," Kiel said, straightening up with effort and a small grunt.

"It would have meant a lot to her," Paul said. "She sent my uncle to Germany after the war to try and locate you. He couldn't find out anything."

"I remember him as a sad young man," Kiel said and lifted a branch, dipping his head over a large pink rose. "It took me years to find a variety of rose that would grow well in this soil. These seem to love it here. What did your mother tell you about our time together?"

The directness of the question caught Paul off guard and he stumbled into his answer. "I was ... surprised. For years she would never talk of her time here, and then she suddenly started to tell me all about coming to Berlin, and you, and your friend Rudy Mueller."

Kiel closed his eyes at the mention of Mueller's name and Paul went on, "Then, after all those years, Germany was all she talked about near the end. It was suddenly very important to her that I know what had happened. She also started telling me things I wasn't sure I wanted to know."

Paul stopped. He felt breathless. Before he could speak again, Kiel said, "What made everything most terrible in those days was the suddenness. It's awful to have a young life cut short, to be forced to grow old, to become a complete adult in a month or two, to have to devise ways of staying alive when you've been assuming that it was your right. That should be one of the luxuries of being young; that one is simply young and will always be so. When I was very young I thought that if older people had managed their lives better, they wouldn't have gotten old."

Kiel stopped and turned to face Paul, asking, "May I ask how old you are?"

Without thinking that his age might prove too revealing, Paul answered, "Thirty-nine," but Kiel didn't seem to notice any significance. Kiel turned left onto a path that curved around the lake. He led the way silently, then stopped at a stone bench near the water and sat, motioning Paul to join him. "This is one of my favorite spots. I think it's the best view of the house and I had a painting made of the scene from here. I have cataracts, so I don't see that well anymore. I can actually see this view better in the painting ... if I get very close. It looks rather pointillist to me from here, or maybe it's Monet I mean. The house was built by an Englishman after the First World War. He married a German baroness and came here to live but, apparently, like Englishmen of his time, could only live in places that looked like home. The English made large parts of the world look very British.

"I knew this house before the war. I was in it once when I was nineteen. I was the pianist in a quartet that played for dances. The owners brought us by train all the way from Berlin, because we played what passed for real American jazz. A watered-down variety, but jazz. I was awed by this place, by all the servants. Help's now rather impossible to get, so I've had to close off many rooms. But I love it. I'll hate leaving it, but it can't be helped." Kiel sighed his regret and Paul couldn't bring himself to ask why Kiel would be leaving.

"Do you mind if we sit here awhile? It's a luxury for me to have a whole day at home."

"Not at all," Paul answered.

"I never get over being surprised at what I've been able to do. For a very long time, I just settled for staying alive. Did Kleber tell you much about our time together?"

"He said he made himself your protector, kept you fed and safe. His version was very self-serving, to say the least."

"I don't mean to be rude, but exactly how much did he squeeze out of you to tell you where I was?"

"Not all that much. No more than it was worth."

"Kleber always got his pound of flesh. He could calculate to a fine degree what something was worth to him or someone else. He had a real talent for using people. Dead or alive, Kleber found some use for everyone. He was only a guard, but he was more clever than many of the officers at getting things ... money, gold, jewels, art. He couldn't tell a bad painting from a good one, just assumed it was valuable if his victim seemed anxious to keep it. The day he ran away from the camp it took him all morning to dredge up the things he'd hidden all over the place. And they were mostly just the smaller valuables. The bigger things he'd already brought to some sister's home.

"What a day. The shelling could be heard in the camp and I should have been elated, but the habit of being a prisoner kept me one. I just milled around like everyone else. We'd been without hope for so long that it was impossible to recognize it. Everything was dangerous to us; even freedom.

"The SS were getting out of Flossenbürg as fast as they could. They fled by rank, the most important off first, of course. Most were willing to settle for saving their skins, but not Kleber. He loaded a wheelbarrow with God knows what plunder, but in one way he'd outsmarted himself: He'd wound a lot of his gold inside a motor. He didn't have time to unwind it all and his last words to me were – and I will never forget his fond farewell – 'You slimy little arse-licker, if you lay a hand on that gold I'll be back and take your balls off a slice at a time.' And off he staggered with his barrow in this very smart suit I'd tailored for him. He should have been a millionaire after the war. I'm glad he's not.

"He described the way he lived in his letters. I thought it suited his soul.

"I'm going on too long. It's age ... and meeting Leda's son, I suspect. Conrad says I just like to talk. He gets very angry with me when I go on about the old days. Says I only upset myself. But the past is very much on my mind these days."

"It was the same with Mother."

"Did it irritate you?"

Paul had to think before he said, "It distressed me, because it upset her. And it all seemed so melodramatic ... the laws, the beatings on the streets, the marching, and the 'Heiling.' I knew I was hearing something important, but wished I didn't have to, wished she hadn't had to live it, or you either."

Kiel nodded, then asked, "How did Kleber look?"

"Awful. That is, he *seemed* in awful shape, but it was hard to tell. The place was so dark and dirty, boxes piled all over. I could barely see him, but I could smell him. He was already drunk when we got there. It all looked so shabby, but Sybella swears she saw a painting by Brueghel just sitting on a chair in the middle of all that squalor. Is that possible?"

"Yes. He had three remarkably good pictures I knew of. There was also an Uccello and a Fantin-Latour. The only reason he knew they had any value was that the people who had owned them had been willing to give their lives for them, and probably did. He told me about everything he took, because he couldn't imagine a time when I wouldn't be helpless. It was safe to tell me anything, because I was just something he used, some nothing. You understand?"

"Yes."

"I hope this isn't too distressing."

"No."

"Kleber was no worse than any of them, but I'm afraid that's much like saying leprosy is no worse than cancer. I once saw Kleber kick a man to death. I don't know what the man's offense was, prisoners weren't capable of anything truly awful. He ordered me to stand and watch as he methodically kicked at the man's head. He was counting how many kicks it took before the man died. He said I would learn something from watching. The sight was terrifying, the sound was worse.

"That night he ordered me to come to him in the kitchen. It was warm there and he liked to be cozy when he took his pleasure. He asked how I had felt when I saw him kicking the man and I didn't dare answer. But he knew me and could see I still felt ill from what I'd seen him do. He said that that was the difference between us: he could command and rule, no matter what it took, while I would remain exactly what I was, but only as long as it suited him to keep me alive. That night he told me that when he'd had enough of me, he would say I'd stolen and have the pleasure of finishing me himself. He said he would kick me to death, too, and it wouldn't take forty-seven kicks to finish the likes of me. I was his *Puppel,* his doll boy, and he could pull my strings any way he wanted.

"As always, I did everything he told me to that night. His murder had aroused him. But I'd stayed alive years before he came to the camp and I knew by then that everything else was beside the point: life first and last, because there was nothing else to want. Kleber might be a murdering monster, but he was life. I could hate him, but I couldn't dispense with him.

"And homosexuals had the hardest time staying alive in the camps. Of all the groups, the ones with the pink triangles were the most likely to die, the most likely to be betrayed, or be given killing labor. The other prisoners hated us as much or more than the SS. If one was homosexual, one could only look to others of one's kind for any sense of humanity. We did our best to look after one another, mourned one another, loved one another ... when we could, when it was safe ... even when it wasn't. I don't mean to say we were all honorable.

"I loved someone there. A man my age, an actor. We rarely even touched one another. They watched the homosexuals closely. We had to sleep with our arms outside the covers, no matter how freezing it got, and the cold killed a lot of us. The irony — if that word's even close — was that the other prisoners were at it all the time. But they were 'real' men and what they did with one another was only a kind of 'temporary accommodation.' I've often wondered if any of them ever loved one another. I loved my friend, didn't just want to use him.

"Near the end of the war he was so terribly sick and frail. Dysentery. We'd been hearing for so long that the Allies were only miles away that I'd stopped paying attention. When death is hours away and help is days away, hope is hateful. It was safest not to expect rescue. I'd have done anything to keep my friend alive. He was the only thing in the world I loved. I was past needing hope, but I still needed love.

"There was medicine in the camp, but the officers were hoarding it. They knew that when the war ended, medicine would be priceless on the black market.

"For years an officer had been after me and I thought, I will help my friend live. I will give myself to that ugly awful man to get the medicine. I went to find the officer, feeling very noble about the sacrifice I was going to make ... my body for the medicine. The ugly officer didn't even stop shuffling through files while I told him he could have me. He carried a file to the stove and started throwing papers on the fire. I said, 'Didn't you hear me, sir?' and he turned a page and said, 'You're too old and scrawny. I could get Conrad Veidt for what that medicine is worth.' Too old? I had been so busy surviving by inches that I hadn't noticed the years. I was over thirty. So, four days before you Americans arrived, my friend died.

"When the Americans got to the camp they came with eight of the SS they'd caught on the road. Those SS claimed they had nothing to do with the camp, but we identified them, which felt very reckless and brave to us, because we still could hardly believe they didn't have the power to murder us. The Americans put the SS to burying the dead. Dear God, there were hundreds and it took days. Can you imagine small mountains of corpses or what looked like corpses? There was so little left of them that seemed human, except for the eyes, and many of their eyes were open, just staring and looking so strangely disinterested. Sometimes live ones were so far gone that they got mixed up with the dead and the only way one could tell was to look carefully at all the chests. They were so thin that you could see their hearts beating under the skin.

"All of us took our badges off before the Americans arrived. The criminals took off their green patches, the Jews their yellow, the Gypsies their brown, emigrants their blue. I took off my pink. They were scattered everywhere. All those bright colors made the ground look as if some festive occasion was going on. When the Americans arrived we were all just prisoners, all equal. Judging by the appalled looks of the Americans when they saw us, we must have been quite a sight. I remember feeling excited and happy, and that scared the devil out of me, because I hadn't felt either in ten years."

Kiel shut his eyes and smiled ruefully, remembering, and said, "The first happy feeling I'd had in years and I was sure I would be punished for it.

"The SS had been burning files for days, but they were such meticulous record keepers that a month of burning wouldn't have been enough. I knew my way around the office, so when they'd cleared off, I went to the office to look for my file and destroy it. It was still there. That's when I found I'd been reported to the police in 1935 by a Lutheran minister. How odd, I thought. What interest would a minister have in me, and how had he known?

"I burned my file. I had no family and no one to return to. I was ten years older, had no past or future, so I decided to see what kind of person I could put together. I found the file of the man I'd loved. He'd been arrested with members of his theatre company for hiding a Jew in their theatre. It was a hero's file, but I destroyed it, too. I burned his file and took the stage name he'd chosen for himself. I became a fictional man with an actor's alias.

"I wound the rest of Kleber's gold around my waist and found some loose clothes to wear over it."

Paul looked back toward the house and thought it an extraordinary story to be listening to in this beautiful setting on this superb day after an excellent lunch. Kiel's cultured calm voice heightened the contrast between the indolent air of the day and the routine horrors he so calmly recounted.

"I haven't talked about any of this in years, but I think about it daily. I don't speak of it with Conrad, perhaps because he's part of my new life. He had nothing to do with Dieter Holtman. And I've kept Helmut Kiel and Dieter Holtman separate. Holtman went up in smoke. I'm sorry you had to find me through Kleber. It would have been so much nicer if your mother could have introduced us, wouldn't it?"

Paul didn't answer and Kiel turned to see why. Paul knew Kiel's question needed an answer. "She never talked of the past, that's why I was surprised when she started telling me about it. She particularly wanted me to know about you, that she had tried to protect you, and how terrible it was for her when she found she couldn't.

"Near the end she wanted me to understand what had made her the person she was. She talked about your apartment in Berlin. She said you pretended to be married."

"That building was gone when I got back there," Kiel said sadly. "I wanted to see where my life had stopped. Like my name, it was gone. But, God knows, I didn't go back to Berlin because I really wanted to. It's where the Americans sent us when they emptied the camp.

"Nothing in Berlin was where I'd left it. There were no landmarks. A third of Berlin was just bombed away, and I just barely managed to get by there. I had the means to have almost anything — I had gold — but I wasn't going to waste it on merely surviving, because I could do that better than most. I'd learned to get by on slightly more than nothing. Civilians needed things. They craved coffee and cigarettes and butter. Plain bread was a luxury for me, even the black market kind they made from sawdust. After the camp, even the awfulness of a bombed-out city wasn't an insuperable problem. I could make do with what came to hand. My real problem was carrying all that gold. Kleber probably told you I made off with his gold wire."

"Yes, that's what he said. I hope you did."

"I had a vague plan for it. Only vague, because I learned in the camp not to make plans. Plans involve having a future. The best I could do when all those different armies were carving up Berlin was try to stay in the hands of the Americans."

Kiel rose and said, "I've kept you too long. I'm being selfish. Sybella will think I'm very rude."

"No, Sybella knows how much I've wanted to meet you. She knows it's important for me to have time with you."

"I don't mean to keep raising a painful subject, but I can't help but wish your mother could be here with us."

Paul nodded and wished she were, too. Leda would have managed this so much better. She would have gone to the heart of the matter, said directly what she had come to say, while here he sat in the pain of self-imposed silence. Would the right moment to speak come? Could he force it? It was hard for Paul to hear Kiel through the white noise of agitation in his own head. How could he speak past all the unspoken words lodged in his throat? And what weight did his own nagging concerns have when balanced against Kiel's account of his chaotic history?

"Let me show you the gazebo. I've been meaning for years to have it moved near the lake. All my years here and there's never been enough time. But let me show you. It's a wonderfully silly thing."

They walked away from the lake and along a path dense with lilac bushes. The gazebo was a Victorian wedding cake of intricately cut moldings and decorative frills in a kind of super-Gothic visual tumble surrounded by concentric circles of pink and purple flowers.

They sat opposite one another in the gazebo and Kiel went on with his reminiscence. He told of getting a new ID card that identified him as Helmut Kiel, the name of the actor he had loved in the camp, of finally making his way to Munich, and of opening his shop there on Maximilianstrasse in 1949.

"It was my first lesson in real money. Munich was still shattered, but there was still money and women wanted dresses. Amazingly, there are always the rich, and if they couldn't pay in money, they could pay in antiques or pictures or jewelry. I used some of the gold to get fabrics from France and some American soldiers were a great help bringing things back from Paris. I became a success as Helmut Kiel.

"It was the second time I'd used any of the gold. The first was an ounce for a man who removed tattoos. I wanted the number the Nazis had engraved on my arm removed. I wanted all of Dieter Holtman gone.

"I'd been a number in the camp for years and I didn't feel like Dieter Holtman anymore and I could barely remember who he was or what he'd wanted as a young man. He played piano, loved fun, kept falling in love. A pleasant young man of no great expectations. But you see, Helmut Kiel was newly made, could be anything he chose to be. I decided how he would walk and talk, what he would like to eat and wear. I had to put someone strong together, someone who could have anything he wanted from life and who could never again be swept away because he was anonymous and had no power or friends. Because I had nothing to lose, I had great courage."

You've just explained my mother, Paul thought, but only nodded to show Kiel he understood.

As if reading Paul's mind, Kiel said, "Your mother was born with her courage, mine was forced on me.

"I'd known for years that your mother had reached America and was a great success. I didn't know about you. I thought of writing her, but the letters I wrote in my head were as long as books and I was afraid to commit the facts of my changed life to paper.

"I once had tickets to go to New York to introduce a new line and I planned to get in touch with her. But the month before I was to leave, two friends of mine were turned back by your immigration people for being gay, and I'd had enough trouble with that for one lifetime, so I canceled the trip. Now I wish I'd taken the chance and gone.

"And now the Americans have come to me again and I'm about to be acquired by an American conglomerate ... shops, factories, trade names, the lot. Hard for me to believe, but it's time for me to stop."

Kiel paused, as if to consider how true that was, then, "Thank God for Conrad. I couldn't face retirement without him. If he weren't in my life I would probably just push on with the business until they carried me out of my office. I want us to have some time for just the two of us. He's been very good for me and he's put up with a lot. I'm not easy and I'm sometimes afraid, now that I have so much to lose. Before him, my experience of loving people was that, if I did, something bad would happen to them, and I sometimes felt that I had brought it on them. I spent years thinking I'd gotten your mother in trouble.

"That day in Berlin when they came and took me from our flat, they beat me and kept asking me to tell them where your mother was. They gave so much energy to seeking out the deviates and those who helped them. I was no hero; I just didn't know, but I was sure they'd found her, that she'd disappeared into a camp, as I had. I had no way to find out.

"I didn't hear of Leda till one night, on one of the outlawed radios, I heard them announce her as 'the famed American pianist Leda Kohl.' American? How could that be? Lord knows what she played, because all I did was cry because my beautiful friend was alive."

Kiel stood and looked at his watch: "I've really been shame-lessly selfish keeping you to myself this long. But having you come is like getting a gift from Leda. I'm touched that she still thought of me for all those years. That means so much to me. I fear it's made me sentimental." Kiel turned away and started down the steps of the gazebo.

Paul followed, noticing how long the shadows now were. The day was running out. He ached to speak and he dropped behind Kiel. If he couldn't say it to Kiel's face he would speak to his back, because he was sure he couldn't bear to see Kiel's reaction, no matter what it might be.

Without turning, Kiel spoke: "I hope you won't mind my asking you not to tell anyone what I've told you. It's important to me to leave my past a secret. I've been indiscreet, because you are Leda's son and telling you was almost like telling her. Though, come to think of it, I don't think I could have burdened her with this."

They again reached the lines of rosebushes near the steps to the house, and Kiel stopped again to examine his prized blooms, moving slowly from bush to bush, giving each his concentrated attention. He said, "These don't last long, once they're picked, but I'd like to send some back with Sybella. These red ones, don't you think? I'll send Bruck down to cut some. I hope the new owners will look after these roses. I must remember to tell them how hard it was to find roses that do well here. I'll take some cuttings with me, of course. Maybe they'll thrive in Switzerland, too. But maybe I shouldn't. If they don't survive it will just pain me. It never does to grip the past too tightly."

Paul wondered how ill he was: What was it? How bad? but only asked, "Why Switzerland?"

"Conrad says I'm being paranoid, but I think they're coming again. Heavens, but that sounds melodramatic when I say it. I just think it's time for them. The haters are gathering again."

"The Nazis could never come back to power."

"No, no. Long black leather coats are out of style. Germany could never do that again; the world knows that act. They'll probably wear business suits this time, but they'll be the same people with the same terrible messages: all the ills in our world are the fault of the godless homosexuals, and nothing is our fault, because we're good God-fearing family people, the *Volk*. They'll say it's God's will to wipe us out or it's for the good of the state or the family or whatever, but it will come down to the same thing: Hate the homosexuals. They say we're weak, but they still think we can overthrow governments, destroy cultures. They don't see the contradiction in their arguments: Imagine weak, powerless people doing all that.

"Besides, Paul, hate is exhilarating. It energizes bored people. And no thought required. It can even be ennobling, if you're doing God's work. Of course, what's never said is that hate is a potent source of power and money, and a splendid rallying point. Just imagine all that's to be had from just organizing hatred. It's a wonder there's not more of it around.

"Time eventually destroys them – it always does – but they'll have done their terrible work. Well, I'm too old for all that. Switzerland is always safe, if you have enough money.

"I understand hate, because it almost destroyed my life. I've had to deal with my own and come to terms. It takes over, because it can feel so good. The hardest thing I ever had to do was learn to forgive everyone everything. And I'm not speaking of saintliness, I'm talking self-preservation."

Kiel stopped and smiled sheepishly at Paul: "Now I've done it. I've been what Conrad calls 'a boring old fart.' Help me down off my soapbox and we'll go back. I do apologize for going on."

Kiel started off while Paul stood, trying to find his voice, the right words, and the courage to say, "I'm your son."

{

"They've stopped again. Mr. Kiel's fussing with the roses. I don't think the flowers have ever been more beautiful. That makes him very happy, but I'm afraid it will make him miss them all the more. I'm the one who's urged him to retire. I hope I've done the right thing. He won't blame me if I haven't, but I pray it will go well for him, be good for both for us." Conrad turned his back on the garden below and walked across the terrace to where Sybella sat. He said, "It's getting late. Are you getting cold? Would you like a drink or something to eat?"

"A drink would be nice," she said, rising and following him into the house.

They went to a small sitting room that was cozy with flowered-print fabrics and simple country furniture. Two deep armchairs faced a large television set. This room didn't have the elegance of the others in the house. It looked comfortably lived-in and a little worn.

Each was grateful for the other's company and had even managed to enjoy their time together. He found her intelligent and eagerly interested, asking informed questions about the furniture and pictures in the house and adding insights from her own store of knowledge. As the day passed, they had begun talking about themselves, opening up to one another about their mutual dilemmas. Both were now anxious for Helmut and Paul to return, even though both feared Paul's intentions and their unknowable outcome.

"Sherry, or something stronger?" Conrad asked.

"Something stronger, I think. A liter of gin would suit me, but I'll settle for Campari-soda."

Conrad laughed and said, "I think it would serve them right to come back and find the two of us drunk. This is not an easy day for us."

"Do you suppose he told him?" she asked, taking her drink from Conrad.

"I've thought about this so much that now I don't know what would be best."

"It may come down to Paul's not being able to stop himself. It couldn't affect Helmut's health, could it?"

"No. The health problems are numerous, none life threatening in itself, but, all together, they make simple things difficult. The worst problem is the cataracts. It's very hard for him not to be able to see well. His whole life has been visual and he sees like an artist. He takes in everything. This house is full of his sense of beauty. It's painful to see him stumble against things or go to pick something up, but miss and break it." His hand stroked his forehead and wiped the frown away.

Sybella rose and went to put her arm around Conrad's shoulder. When she felt him relax she stepped back, put her hand under his chin, and smiled, saying, "Oh, shit, Conrad, break out the gin."

He laughed and said, "Whatever happens, I hope we'll see you again."

"I'd like that."

They snapped to rigid attention when they heard Paul's and Dieter's voices in the hall, and Sybella and Conrad exchanged worried glances and assumed poses each hoped would look nonchalant.

Kiel gestured Paul into the room ahead of him, saying, "My apologies for neglecting you both. I lost track of time. I'm afraid I've monopolized Paul, Sybella. Paul may tell you what we said, if he wishes." He took Sybella's hand and said, affectionately, "I've asked Bruck to cut you some roses to take back with you. Now I must ask you all to excuse me. I've missed my nap and I'm feeling rather tired."

Conrad started toward Kiel, but Kiel waved him back: "No, please. Stay and look after our guests." He turned to Sybella and Paul and said, "It was very kind of you to come. Now, if you'll excuse me."

Paul moved toward Kiel, who seemed suddenly uncertain on his feet, but stopped, realizing that help might not be welcome. Instead he stepped to Sybella's side and pulled her to him, hurting her with the pressure of his grip.

As Mr. Kiel stopped at the door, Paul said, "Thank you very much for everything."

⸘

The gates swept shut behind them and Paul stopped the car, its nose halfway onto the empty road.

He sat with his head back against the seat, his eyes closed, his arms crossed tightly over his chest, and his hands jammed into his armpits. "I feel cold."

She watched anxiously as a shiver convulsed him.

"I'm going to be sick," he gasped and bolted from the car. She flung open her door to follow. He fled up the road with surprising speed, then stopped abruptly and fell to his knees.

She cursed her high heels as she stumbled to where he now sat, his knees against his chest. To her surprise, he looked calm, but she still asked, "Are you all right?" as she crouched by him, placing her hand on his forehead.

He said, "I think I'm breathing for the first time since we got here. Why aren't things ever the way you imagine they'll be? Reality always screws up what I imagine." He took her hand from his shoulder and folded it in his. "Thank you for being there. What a day. I'm just grateful I didn't act like a madman or throw up while he was telling me about the camp. Christ, it was like some guided tour through hell."

He sat up straight and said, "Are you hungry? Of course you are. Hard to believe, but I'm starved. Is there someplace on the way back that's any good?"

"There's an inn near Holzkirchen I've been to, if I can find it."

He stood and brushed himself clean of grass. "I'm too old to run like that. I could kill myself. I'm too old for a lot of things. Do you ever feel that way?"

She nodded.

ƨ

They drove in silence for a while and then Paul began to tell Sybella Kiel's story, which took most of the drive to the inn.

All Sybella could think to say, over and over, was, "My God."

"There are a lot of similarities between my mother and him. They both turned out to be strong people. Is that a German trait? I mean, is there something in the German character that lets them push on through things that terrible? They not only survived, they became successes."

"Being German doesn't explain people like your mother and Helmut, or even Hitler."

"You're strong," he said.

"I'm not strong, just stubborn," she said and amended, "No, perhaps just tenacious."

They drove a little longer in silence and, when she could no longer stand being discreet, she asked, "Did you?"

"You mean did I tell him?"

She poked his shoulder. "You know I do."

Paul thought back to the last moments in the garden, then said, "No. I can't believe I came so close to telling him and stopped. We were just about to go up the steps from the garden and I said, 'Helmut, there's something I think I must tell you.' He stopped and looked at me, but he heard Conrad's voice from the terrace. He looked up at him with such intensity and then he smiled. When he looked back at me he said, 'I'm lucky, Paul. No, I'm blessed. Conrad is a blessing.' He gave me the nicest smile and I knew I couldn't tell him. Instead, I said, 'I'm sorry my mother never found you.' He said he was, too, so he could thank her for trying to save his life."

"It must have been very hard not to tell him."

"Oh, yes. Maybe someday, if we get to know one another better — if I give it some time — maybe then. But I doubt it. When we were walking back to the house, he asked me about you and I said you'd been wonderful for me. He said he understood that, that having someone to love made all the difference.

"I know he's my father, but Conrad was right. Knowing he's my father doesn't make me love him and it wouldn't mean he'd love me. I might be a son, but I wasn't sure I'd be much of a blessing.

"I'm not sure what I mean by this, but when he turned to me and I was going to tell him, I thought that if I said, 'I'm your son,' it might be the most terribly selfish thing I'd ever done."

Paul

Chapter 8

It took cajoling just short of threat for Sybella to get Paul to return to the United States.

"Accept the degree in honor of Helmut's memory," she said. "Conrad would like that. Your mother would have been pleased to see how much good came of her money. Besides, your being there will tell the school that you're still interested in the research and not just some remote benefactor."

Paul grumped, but agreed, and once the plane from Munich landed in New York, Paul was glad he had come.

As they came out of the Midtown Tunnel into Murray Hill and moved toward Fifth Avenue, Paul examined the streets, shook his head, and *tsk*ed. "I can't believe the changes. The city looks so tattered and scarred. Look at the filth in the streets, that ugly scrawl on the buildings."

To Sybella, who had never been to America, some of the city looked startlingly beautiful and other parts ugly and abandoned. However, the hotel they arrived at might have been on Munich's Maximilianstrasse.

They would stay only overnight at the Peninsula. They had planned to walk to dinner and see some sights, but after reading a pamphlet in their room that suggested precautions tourists should take against crime, decided to eat dinner in the hotel, then have the hotel hire a car and driver to take them past Paul's old home and see some of the city's other attractions.

Paul had been uneasy about seeing his old home and somewhat relieved to find the sight of the obviously well-tended building didn't draw his mind or feelings back to times he had no interest in reclaiming. Somehow, the sight confirmed his pleasure in his present life with Sybella in Munich.

At six the next morning a car picked them up for the drive to Veritas College in Vermont where Paul was to be awarded an honorary doctorate in history, not for any accomplishment in the field, but for the half million dollars that he and Helmut Kiel had agreed to use to establish "pink triangle" research almost twenty years earlier.

They had tried giving the money to a German university, but hadn't been able to find any takers, because Helmut and Paul had insisted the money be used only to underwrite research into the fate of homosexuals in Hitler's Germany. Their search among American universities found these institutions equally reluctant. It was Karly who found a school willing, even eager, to accept the money and carry out their intentions. Veritas was a small college founded by Quakers that lay between Rutland and Montpelier, and just east of Braintree.

As they passed fiery autumn trees, Paul and Sybella were awed and delighted to have chosen such a perfect time to visit New England.

The Helmut Kiel Trust had flourished, thanks to the school's young investment banker who had put half the money in "widows and orphans" stocks and the rest in emerging computer software companies. The money financed field trips to Germany and the copying of countless court records used to construct the paper trail that led from civil arrests to the camps and, too often, back to jails. Over the years, a few German researchers were given money and became associates of the Veritas people in the hunt for dependable information.

But the trail was growing old and cold as elderly gays who had survived the concentration camps died. Even in the early days of the research, it was almost impossible to find surviving gays willing to talk of their experiences. Another frustration of the work was lack of interest on the part of book publishers and other media in tens of thousands dead or murderously punished gays. As one of the researchers put his frustration, "Because they were gay, their persecution has become a treachery hidden within a lie wrapped in silence."

As the trust was now generating more money than it could use effectively, Paul had been asked to talk to its director, Liam O'Donnell, about diversifying the purposes of the trust into other areas of study.

The ride was proving so charming that Paul almost regretted the sight of the school. They stopped in front of the Fleming Building as instructed and found they were being awaited, as five people hurried down the steps and toward the car to greet them. Sybella was herded off by the three women for a tour of the small campus and Paul was taken away to meet with the trust's director and hear his report on the state of research. On the way, the day's busy itinerary was laid out for Paul.

Paul was introduced to Liam O'Donnell and left with him. O'Donnell looked as Irish as his name, with red hair, freckled pink skin, and a puckish smile. O'Donnell was quick and concise about the state of the research, then Paul raised the question of the excess money accumulating in the trust. O'Donnell said, "We've pretty much got the field covered and still can't spend all the money. It's the Microsoft and Intel stock. Hard to imagine a trust with too much money, Mr. Howe. If you want to spread some of it around, you could endow a chair, offer scholarships. Our audiovisual department is pretty desperate to upgrade. As to Gay Studies, I have some ideas. I've put recommendations and costs in a memo to you." He handed Paul a slim blue binder. "No rush. Read it and tell me what you think."

Paul asked, "Have you considered something to do with AIDS?"

"Yes, but I'm not sure where we could do important work that's not being done. It might be best to simply funnel money to people already in the field. I know I'm at risk of putting myself out of a job but, as we've defined the trust's purpose, this work has an end. Beyond a point it's just minutiae and, frankly, not the kind of fussy work I'd like to give more of my life to. It's about fifty years since that war ended. That we were able to do as much as we did is a wonder, and all thanks to you and Mr. Kiel."

O'Donnell checked his watch. "I've got to get you over to lunch, but I'd like you to see the publicty we've gotten on your receiving the doctorate." He began taking clippings from a folder and handing them to Paul. "Coverage in every local newspaper, as far away as Albany.

"We're a small school, Mr. Howe, but we have a fine reputation, so when we honor someone, the event has a certain distinction. Most of the papers even carried a description of the trust's work. More press than we've gotten in the last two years."

O'Donnell rose. "Now, we'd better get on our way. I'll be skinned if I make you late."

O'Donnell sped ahead of Paul, out the building, and across the grass, Paul puffing along behind. Paul was again struck by the beauty of the day and the setting, and wished his hosts had planned a picnic.

Lunch was punctuated by several toasts to the distinguished visitors from Munich, and Sybella and he were then taken to the auditorium where students already filled most of the seats. Paul felt his age as he looked down at the students from the stage.

The dignitaries of the occasion were lined up on folding chairs on the high stage that looked over the steeply raked auditorium and toward the door that led onto the school's central quad.

There were to be three speeches. The first was lengthy and earnest, and Paul fought the torpor of the lunch and wine. The second speech began on a high laudatory note, then faltered into silence when the blast of noise came crashing into the room. First there was the screech of horns blasted in discord, then a voice given size and menace by a loud-hailer shrilled: "Faggots go home! Faggots go home!" Loud voices chorused their hate, then truck horns began blaring. Everyone in the room was briefly frozen, then began to rise uncertainly, some moving warily into the aisles. A student ran to throw open the auditorium's doors.

From the vantage of the stage, Paul saw pickup trucks ganged outside. Some men stood on top of them waving rifles and shotguns. Other men and women stood beside the trucks holding crudely made signs and flags. It was the flags that were as heart-stopping as a pointed gun. They were the red, black, and white swastikas of the Nazi Reich.

Paul couldn't read the signs from where he stood, but the flags blazed their message, their colors fresh and unfaded after all these decades. New flags for old hate, still vitally emblematic of the disease.

"Faggots go home! Faggots go home."

Some of the demonstrators laughed with the pleasure of taunting children, as if greatly amused by a game.

Paul heard someone asking for a camera or camcorder and understood the man's intention to record the invasion. Someone else was saying, "We've called the state police." Paul looked to where Sybella stood among faculty and students. She didn't look afraid; she was weeping.

Paul wanted a closer look at the invaders, wanted to read what the placards said. All Paul could think as he hurried up the aisle was how grateful he was that Leda and Helmut weren't here and could never know.

As Paul was about to step outside, O'Donnell grabbed his arm and pulled him back. "Please don't go out there, Mr. Howe. They've got guns."

"They wouldn't dare use them."

"You have been away a long time."

"I want to see what their signs say."

"Nothing new, I'm sure. Ugly, but not original."

O'Donnell kept his restraining hand on Paul's arm with such pressure that the spot grew damp.

Helmut Kiel had said they couldn't come marching under their old banner for malice, that the new monsters would need a new symbol, but there they stood in the sun, the brilliant autumn foliage for a backdrop, the ugly past resurrected and recast with Americans.

The dissonance of horns and screamed slogans was finally joined by the wail of troopers' cars arriving.

Paul stepped outside and saw four troopers moving among the invaders, motioning them off the tops of their trucks, pointing them back into their vehicles. It went smoothly, as if everyone knew the drill.

Paul saw a trooper rest his hand on a trucker's shoulder. The trooper said something to the man and they shared a laugh, heads and hands gesturing toward the auditorium. Then, smiling, the trooper pushed the man's gun to point toward the ground and gestured his friend on his way.

All Paul could think to say was, "Jesus!"

"I'm afraid it was the publicity we were so proud of, Mr. Howe. Honey for the flies. Now they'll all go and get drunk, and brag about how brave they are, how they're the real Americans."

"When they're brought up on charges, if you need a witness, I'll stay."

"The school is regarded as an oddity in this area. Education is suspect. The school won't want bad blood with the town, so the short answer on charging these fools is: No."

"Then how will you keep this from being repeated?"

"A good question for which I don't have an answer."

The last of the trucks pulled off the quad, leaving the trash of their signs, beer cans, and liquor bottles behind, and grass scarred by revved tires. They'd taken their flags.

The day was still brilliant, but had been drained of pleasure, as if some vandal had thrown ink on a beautiful picture.

Someone moved behind Paul and Liam and said, "We can breathe easy. People like that can be frightening, but it's hard to take such rabble seriously. Stupid, uneducated louts. Just the kind those people are up here recruiting all the time. Diseased minds."

"In very healthy bodies," O'Donnell said.

The speaker nodded soberly and moved away.

Much to his surprise, Paul found himself still clutching the rolled scroll he'd been given. It was badly crushed and damp with sweat. He said, "Let's go clean up their mess." They moved down to the open area, started picking up the debris, and were soon joined by others eager to restore order.

Paul flipped through the placards he'd gathered and said with disgust, "Christ, who needs Germany, when we can grow our own Nazis?

"My mother and father barely survived people like that. So, let's not be too quick to put the trust's money elsewhere, Mr. O'Donnell. This time, let's think of how to spend it before the fact. We've been unearthing the past; it would have been better if there'd been nothing that needed to be dug up.

"What is it the Jews say about the Holocaust? 'Never again'? A good slogan. But what's to be done, and how? And with whom do gay people make common cause?"

"I've no idea."

"Neither have I, but we should start doing something, and quickly. I can't think of anything more terrible than being one of the good men who do nothing."

Other books of interest from
ALYSON PUBLICATIONS

THE MEN WITH THE PINK TRIANGLE, by Heinz Heger, $9.00. For decades, history ignored the Nazi persecution of gay people. Only with the rise of the gay movement in the 1970s did historians finally recognize that gay people, like Jews and others deemed "undesirable," suffered enormously at the hands of the Nazi regime. Of the few who survived the concentration camps, only one ever came forward to tell his story. His true account of those nightmarish years provides an important introduction to a long-forgotten chapter of gay history.

THE HUSTLER, by John Henry Mackay, $8.00. Gunther is fifteen when he arrives alone in the Berlin of the 1920s. Soon he discovers the boys of Friedrich Street, and the men who stroll by and speak with them – and one man in particular, the young Hermann Graff, who falls hopelessly in love with Gunther. Mackay wrote *The Hustler* in 1926. Today, this first English translation combines a poignant love story with a colorful portrayal of the gay subculture that thrived in Berlin sixty years ago.

A HISTORY OF SHADOWS, by Robert C. Reinhart, $6.00. Through the eyes of four older gay men, Robert Reinhart vividly depicts what it was like to grow up gay in America a half century ago, and to live in the closet during the Depression, World War II, the McCarthy witch-hunts, and the stormy sixties.

BECOMING VISIBLE, edited by Kevin Jennings, $10.00. Drawing from both primary and secondary sources, this reader covers more than two thousand years of history and a diverse range of cultures. Designed for classroom use, *Becoming Visible* contains classroom activities and curriculum suggestions to help teachers incorporate this material into existing classes. The readings are suitable for age levels from ninth grade through college, but the book will also be welcomed by general readers seeking insight into gay and lesbian history.

OUT OF ALL TIME, by Terry Boughner, $7.00. Historian Terry Boughner scans the centuries and picks out scores of the past's most celebrated gay, lesbian, and bisexual personalities. From ancient Egypt to the twentieth century, from Alcibiades to Willa Cather, we discover a part of history that has too often been censored or ignored. Each chapter is imaginatively illustrated by Michael Willhoite.

GAY MEN AND WOMEN WHO ENRICHED THE WORLD, by Thomas Cowan, trade paper, $9.00. Growing up gay or lesbian in a straight culture, writes Thomas Cowan, challenges the individual in special ways. Cowan has written lively accounts of forty men and women who offered outstanding contributions in different fields, ranging from mathematics and military strategy to art, philosophy, and economics. Each chapter is amusingly illustrated with a caricature by Michael Willhoite.

THE TROUBLE WITH HARRY HAY, by Stuart Timmons, $13.00. This complete biography of Harry Hay, known as the father of gay liberation, sweeps through forty years of the gay movement and nearly eighty years of a colorful and original American life. Hay went from a pampered childhood, through a Hollywood acting career and a stint in the Communist party before starting his life's work in 1950 when he founded the Mattachine Society, the forerunner of today's gay movement.

WE CAN ALWAYS CALL THEM BULGARIANS, by Kaier Curtin, $10.00. In this landmark study, theater historian Kaier Curtin charts the struggle to portray the lives of gay men and lesbians on the American stage. Despite virulent homophobia, many plays with gay and lesbian characters did appear on Broadway in the first half of the twentieth century, and Curtin documents the controversies sparked by these works.

SUPPORT YOUR LOCAL BOOKSTORE

Most of the books described here are available at your nearest gay or feminist bookstore, and many of them will be available at other bookstores. If you can't get these books locally, order by mail using this form.

Enclosed is $_____ for the following books. (Add $1.00 postage if ordering just one book. If you order two or more, we'll pay the postage.)

1._____

2._____

3._____

name:_____

address:_____

city:_____state:_____zip:_____

ALYSON PUBLICATIONS
Dept. J-54, 40 Plympton St., Boston, MA 02118
After June 30, 1996, please write for current catalog.